The Veil of Sorrow

For Lisa

The Veil of Sorrow

by

Crystal Michallet-Romero

Crystal M R

7/6/2017

Cover art by Linda Callaghan

http://calliweb.freewebhost.co.nz

Cover photo, Angel of Mourning, courtesy of Jessica Michallet-Romero

Interior design by Aidana WillowRaven

Original publication 2009 by P.D. Publishing

Second edition 2015

ISBN-13: 978-1508642046

ISBN-10: 1508642044

Dedicated to my wife, Jessica Michallet-Romero

Part 1

Chapter 1

I woke early from a restful slumber. Before I opened my eyes I heard a slight rustling, but when I opened my lids the servant had vanished from the room. To my surprise the tray containing the remnants of my dinner delights had been removed. In its place rested a steaming pot. I would have pondered this further if the aromatic scent of tea had not enticed me. Unlike the prior night, I did not hear the familiar lock at my door and knew that I was now allowed my freedom.

Without ado, I rose from the comfortable bed and made haste to dress. Between sips of the delectable warmth, I quickly washed and groomed myself, choosing one of the few proper dresses that I owned. I wish I could have taken the morning to explore the château, but I remembered Madame's instructions and took my new, clean steno pad, a fresh jar of ink, and my pens in hand. Now would be the first day of my full employment.

I left my room and made my way down the winding staircase. I heard the rustling of servants and walked to their location. The room I entered was not a dining room but a parlor of such grandeur it took away my breath. The furniture was exquisitely carved rosewood and covered with velvet cushions. Like my room, there was a large fireplace. The only difference between the two was that this one was lined with exotic green marble. Over the mantle hung a huge oil painting of the most beautiful woman I had ever seen, her sharp grey eyes captivated me. Sitting neatly in a chair, the elegant woman's poise was both regal and confident. A ruby red dress and jeweled necklace offset her sable hair. Through the oils I could see the delicate silk fabric of her dress and knew she was a grand woman.

As I gazed upon the image I wondered at her identity. Could she be an ancestor of Madame Faivre? Even as I thought this I doubted it, for there was no family resemblance between the two.

"She is striking is she not?" Madame Faivre's voice pulled me away from my examination.

"Yes, quite," I replied as I lowered my eyes, warmth covering my cheeks. I was not certain if I had overstepped my boundaries by admiring such an exquisite portrait, or for experiencing the feelings the image elicited within me. When the elderly lady appeared as spellbound as I, I grew calm.

"She is the original mistress of the house, the Lady Laurensa Catherine de la Fontaine," the older woman said as her nurse wheeled her toward the fireplace.

I had never thought that I had seen such devotion, such emotions as I now saw this older woman demonstrate before this single painting. As she looked lovingly at the image, I glanced up and gazed further. I could not help but notice Lady de la Fontaine's high cheek bones and delicate red rose colored lips. The healthy glow of life surrounded this grand lady and within her eyes was an air of mischievous happiness. When I turned my attention once more to her stunning eyes, it felt as if the image was staring down upon me, gauging and judging me for what, I do not know. At this horrific thought, I inhaled deeply and averted my gaze. Sensing my unease, Madame Faivre smiled as she signaled to her nurse. The nurse began to wheel her to the waiting table.

"Come, I did not bring you here to gaze upon the paintings," Madame Faivre stated as she turned her attention to the breakfast that was laid out. "There will be ample time at a later date to take you on a tour of the château."

"Of course, Madame, please forgive me," I stammered then began to prepare the tools of my trade for the diction expected of me. Before I could remove the new ink jar from my pocket, Madame Faivre interrupted my actions.

"Not now, dear. Come and sit with me. Enjoy this meal before we begin our work," she said, as a male servant held a chair for me.

I was startled to see a different man. Almost as tall as Amadieu but with light brown hair, this servant had a moustache above his lips. Sensing my curiosity, he smiled slightly as he nodded a greeting before stepping away.

"Have you met Frederic?" Madame Faivre asked as she motioned to the young man.

"No, I only met Amadieu," I said in hopes of masking my surprise.

"Ah, yes, Amadieu. He rests in the day and works in the evenings," Madame Faivre explained.

"Indeed, how...unconventional." I glanced around the room at the handful of servants waiting to serve their mistress. All held a rosy glow about their cheeks and their flesh, unlike the prior night's servants, were colored with a healthy hue.

"It is a new way of organization. We," Madame Faivre glanced at the servants, "find that it suits our needs."

I could not help but notice the slight smiles and knowing glances of the servants and wondered what it meant. But at the smell of freshly baked croissants, cooked eggs, and an assortment of colorful fruits, combined with the sounds of my empty stomach, I turned my attention to the morning meal.

As I ate I listened with rapt attention to the words of my host and employer. Since I was not expected to take down her words, I do not have an exact chronicle of this discussion. However, it should suffice to say that Madame Faivre spoke of the weather, the end of winter, how lovely her garden is in the spring, and the number of rooms in the château. She spoke as well about various balls and celebrations she had hosted in this grand home over the years.

When the meal was complete and the servants began to clear away the table, Madame Faivre signaled for her nurse. I noticed the unspoken commands exchange and as the nurse began to move her mistress closer to the fireplace, I took up my steno pad and fountain pens and followed close behind. Frederic lifted the fragile body and gently placed her in the high-backed chair. As the nurse covered the woman's legs with a warm blanket, I moved to a nearby chair with a small desk beside it. I placed the new jar of ink and fountain pens next to it then settled into the chair with the steno pad in my lap.

"Lady Faivre, you hired me for a purpose?" I spoke in a soft and respectful tone.

As if to wave away my words, she shook her head negatively. "Please, Mademoiselle Dupuin, I am no *Lady*. She," her withered hand pointed upward to the image which seemed to watch our every move. "She is a *Lady*," her voice stated with conviction. "I, on the other hand, am a commoner, like you."

"Beg pardon, Madame Faivre, I meant no offense."

"No offense taken." She smiled warmly at me. "But now, to the purpose of your employment." Madame Faivre's voice grew soft as she settled in. "I wish for you to record my words, to chronicle my life for future posterity."

I listened closely to her and grew suddenly alarmed. "You are not ill, Madame?"

"Ill?" the old woman looked surprised as a smile crossed her lips. "If the illness is mortality, then yes, I am ill." Her words brought a slight chuckle from the servants and an embarrassed blush to my features.

"Child, I am old and one day will not be here. I have no progeny. All I have is my life, and I wish for it to be chronicled. You come highly regarded, and therefore I would like for you to complete this task."

I looked at the woman and realized for the first time her true frailty. Her hands, while resting on her lap, shook from slight tremors. A face both regal and elegant held the look of one close to the end of her life. I understood then what her designs would be and why I was hired.

"Very well, Madame." I smiled tenderly upon her as I readied myself for dictation. I carefully opened the jar of black ink, steadied my pad upon my lap, and dipped an iridium tip into the black liquid before turning my gaze to the aged woman.

"I begin this tale from the beginning, and by the end of it you may think it untrue. You may wonder if I speak folly, or if my accounts are that of a mad old woman." Her voice trailed off.

"No, Madame, I assure I will hold no judgment."

"Of course, of course." Madame Faivre nodded and then she turned her gaze to the fire's flame. "Then we shall begin at the beginning so that you will know from whence I came."

13 February, morning – The recollections of Madame Agnes (Nina) Brigitte Faivre.

"It began in the winter, as all things tend to do. I was the eldest daughter of three, and my father was a banker in Annecy. We were of modest means, but this in no way meant that we were lacking. In fact up until my tale begins I never had a want." Madame Faivre's voice became softer and more solemn. "All of my needs and desires were cared for and then mama died." Her dark wizened eyes stared into the fire's flame as if recalling the pain from long ago.

"Papa was devastated, for he could not live without her. She brought him happiness and made him whole, and soon after mama joined the angels, papa followed. It was a hard time for us children, a devastating time. We knew nothing of the world and its heartaches. All we knew was that our life would never be the same again." Madame Faivre's voice flittered in a delicate harmony as she recalled her life.

"My brother and sisters were separated from me, taken to an orphanage, but there was a different fate in store for me." Bitterness edged her voice. "For me, my papa's close friend and business partner had something entirely different in mind. You see, although my papa was a banker, he left a great deal of debt to the business. In order to pay off the debt, his partner thought it would be a good idea that I should be wed. 'Only the best of marriages would do,' he told me. But I soon discovered what he considered the best. For him, best meant the wealthiest, and that is how I ended up leaving everything I knew in Annecy."

Madame Faivre's voice grew solemn as her eyes slightly closed while she told her tale from long ago...

*****

Nina, as she was called by her family and friends, felt the bitter cold biting through her cape. Despite having a coverlet over the window, the harsh rain seeped into the coach and drenched the floorboard. In a delicate manner, she picked up her feet hoping her shoes would not become drenched. When the coach jerked, she reached for the walls to stabilize herself. Through her long, dark lashes she cast Monsieur Pétain as evil and eye as she could, yet doubted it had any effect on his disposition. Just as he had been when her father was alive, Monsieur Pétain was intent on his own affairs. Right now that meant making it to Lyon by tomorrow.

As her life began to unravel before her, Nina did not care about her future. She only lamented her past. She mourned for the loss of her mother who had died of consumption, and later, her father dying of grief. Now she mourned the loss of her younger brother and sisters. She wondered where they had been sent and what would happen to them. Each time she questioned Monsieur Pétain, he answered in short, clipped phrases, or not at all. Once, when she threw herself upon his mercy, his patience ran thin and she received the back of his hand. From that point forward she knew to be cautious of her queries lest they bring out the man's temper.

With each jerk of the cabin, she glared at the man who seemed impervious to her emotions. By the light of a single lamp he pulled out a map and began to read it, then, filled with anger he looked at his time piece before mumbling under his breath, "We shall never make it on time. Damn these stops."

"Monsieur Pétain, won't we be able to rest for the night?" Nina implored as the aches and pains of her body accosted her.

"No," came his gruff reply as he examined the map again. "We have already lost too much time. The agreement was to have you in Lyon by midday. At the rate we're going we'll be lucky to reach it at all!" he exclaimed just as the coach jerked to a stop. There was a bit of commotion outside as the coachman unharnessed the fatigued horses to exchange them for a fresh pair from the inn. Nina watched the man through the thin slits in the curtain and felt a pang of empathy for his plight. With a family to tend to, a wife with a babe on the way, this poor soul took them for the promised coins awaiting him at the end of their journey. Before a melancholy settled over Nina a knock was heard at the door.

"Maybe now we can get some answers," Monsieur Pétain said as he opened the door to see a villager.

The man was short and stout, like the people of the region. He wore a woolen cap and thick coat. Wrapped around each hand were wooly gloves to keep his digits warm. "Monsieur, perhaps you and your daughter would like to come into my inn for the night and rest out the storm?" the man asked in a pleasant tone.

"She is not my daughter, and no, we do not wish to spend the night. We must make haste to Lyon. Tell me, if you please, is this route still open?" Monsieur Pétain pointed at something on the map.

The villager inspected the scribbles carefully by the pale lamps light before turning a fearful gaze upon the man. "Yes, Monsieur, but," the man stammered, "I would not advise it. There are two ways to reach Lyon, down the road you travel now, and by the river. I would humbly suggest that Monsieur remains on this road if he wishes to get there safely."

"Safely be damned! I need to get there by midday tomorrow. I know that this second route is quicker. What I need to know is if the road is still high above the river?" His temper caused the poor villager to flinch as he gazed at the map.

"Yes, Monsieur, this one is well above the water lines, the roads are not yet flooded." The man hesitated as he glanced from Nina to her well-dressed guardian. "However, for the sake of Mademoiselle, it is better to avoid this route. There are things in this world that defy understanding. For her sake, for yours, avoid the route along L'Isère River lest you wish to meet *Celle qui pleure*," he whispered sharply. His eyes darted to the shadows and then he quickly crossed himself.

"Monsieur, what is *Celle qui pleure*?" Nina could not help but ask.

"No." He shook his head, refusing to speak more. However, Nina saw an excited gleam in his eye, and he leaned forward conspiratorially. "Why, it is a spirit of a woman from long ago. No one knows where she came from, but many have seen her. Some say that she went mad and murdered her children in the river. When she realized what she had done, she drowned herself in the current. Now her spirit wanders along the bank calling out for her beloved infants. Some have seen her to this day, a beautiful woman dressed in white wandering along the river's edge searching and crying for her babies," the man said.

Before Nina's fear could take control, a gruff woman's voice interrupted the innkeeper.

"Bah, there is more to the *Celle qui pleure* than that," the innkeeper's wife grumbled as she pushed him aside and began to replace Nina's drenched blankets with warm, dry ones. "The apparition was once a woman, flesh and blood like you and I, mademoiselle," the woman explained as she tucked Nina under the heap of blankets. "The men would like to say she was plagued with hysteria." She cast an evil glance at her husband as if he were to blame. "We women know better. The Celle qui pleure did not have a weak and feeble mind, as some like to say, nor was she a harlot. She was simply a woman, who gave her love to the wrong man. In the end, the scoundrel left her alone, shamed, and with three children to fend for. In her desperation she did the unthinkable." They innkeeper's wife looked downward as if the story were dear to her heart.

Nina leaned forward in the blankets. "Madame, what happened next?"

"No one knows exactly what happened that night, but the next morning her body was found floating down near the next village and the bodies of her children were discovered along the river bed. All were dead, drowned by the hands of their mother some said. Their little bodies were horribly mangled in various parts as if the flesh had been eaten by the feral beasts of the woods.

"And now she is a ghost wandering along the river's edge?" Nina whispered in fear.

"Bah, foolish stories to scare the wits out of girls." Monsieur Pétain chortled as he waved away the villagers words.

"Monsieur, it would be unwise to mock what you do not know," the innkeeper's wife warned before turning to Nina. "Aside from the horror of her actions, no one gave it any thought until one month later when a mysterious figure was seen walking near the river's edge. A woman of uncommon beauty moved as if floating on air. Her ethereal form wandered to and fro near the riverbank as if seeking something lost. She was dressed in the colors of a heavenly angel, her long white gown floating in the air like the leaves on a tree. Those who survived the spectre's encounters talked of seeing anguish and pain in the woman's face as she mourned for her lost babes," the woman said softly.

"Monsieur, you must believe my wife." The innkeeper pushed past his wife and turned toward Monsieur Pétain "I myself have seen those few who have survived their encounter with the *Celle qui pleure*. Their mad ramblings spoke of the ghost's wailing cries as her cold, unearthly grasp reached for them. Those unlucky enough to escape her clutches were driven to madness and were sent to the lunatic asylum. It is not certain if all the bodies found along the bank are those of her design, but no one living thinks twice. For only an evil like the *Celle qui pleure* could drown her victim so quickly or with such ease. Or, at least, that is how the story is told."

He finished in a hushed whisper. "Although my wife is prone to theatrics, Monsieur, I assure you that there are strange things amiss. I implore you again, please come into my inn to rest. We can give you both warm broth and nice warm beds."

Nina's eyes were wide with fright as she listened. Before the fear could take hold, she heard the scoffing of her guardian. With a wave of his hand he dismissed the village's words and leaned back, folding the map.

"Nonsense, complete nonsense. I am a man of science and do not believe in the hobgoblins of the past," Monsieur Pétain said, just as a crash of thunder was heard in the distance. "Please tell our driver the way to the second road once the horses are ready. I wish to make haste immediately."

"But Monsieur, even if you do not believe in ghosts, surely you would rather travel when you can see. There are markers in the road and if missed, you might end up at the château of the Comtesse de la Fontaine. It, Monsieur, is an even darker and more forbidding place to be stranded than with *Celle qui pleure*," the villager whispered the warning.

"Never you mind about us. Please explain the directions to our driver so that we may be on our way." Monsieur Pétain pushed the man away and closed the door against the wind and rain. "Imagine that, losing out on our contract over a silly superstition," he mocked.

Once the fresh horses were hitched, the coachman climbed on top of their vehicle. Nina peeked through the drawn shade. Through the blanket of rain she saw the villager as he stood by his wife's side. With an expression of sorrow, the woman silently made the sign of the cross as her gaze turned downward in silent prayer.

"You'll see," Monsieur Pétain said. "As soon as you are safe in the abode of your betrothed, you'll feel better. Once you say your vows and are his wife, you will not even think twice about this spectral woman. Mark my words, young lady. Once you are married then all of my... I mean, your troubles will be forgotten," he stated right before the sound of the coachman's whistle and the smack of his whip sent the team of horses on their way toward the road along L'Isère River.

With a desolate sigh, Nina pulled the blanket closer around her body. She considered what awaited her in Lyon. There was a husband with wealth enough to pay off all of her father's debts and make Monsieur Pétain a rich man. If he was old or young, kind or cruel, none of this mattered because Nina knew she was powerless against the forces that now surrounded her. To them, she was mere chattel to be bought and sold by the will of men.

As if the storms had read Nina's mind, a loud clap of thunder sounded in the distance. From somewhere near the coach, a flash of light shot through the air and crackled on the top of a nearby tree. The horses responded as though struck directly in the rump. Each reared up in fear, tearing down the muddy road without any guidance from the coachman. Each time the coach landed hard against the ground, Nina held on tight and closed her eyes. Although not overly religious, she sent forth a silent prayer for their fast journey.

13 February, evening – Diary of Mademoiselle Cecilia Natashia Dupuin

I cannot believe the modest beginning of my employer. Madame Faivre appears such an elegant woman. Her bearing and mannerisms speak of refinement, yet if her words are true, her humble beginnings were at odds to her current position.

Today we worked all day, Madame dictated her words and I, an excellent stenographer, wrote them down. On many occasions I found myself startled by her recounting, for which she would stop her narration to assure me of this or that. We stopped a few times in order that Madame and I could take care of nature.

Halfway through the day we had a break where my employer had to be away on business, and I lunched alone. When she returned she appeared invigorated and ready to continue her dictation.

I had so hoped that we could have finished her tale at a different place and time, perhaps after knowing if her carriage made it to her betrothed or if they ran into the spectre. I wondered that if she did, how she managed to escape its evil clutches. There were so many questions whirling in my mind yet, sadly, my job for the day was completed by sunset. The Madame had fallen asleep in her chair. When the servants noticed, they were very kindly and gently gathered the dear woman up and carried her, like a babe, from the room.

I spent the night alone in my room again. Amadieu brought a tray of delicious delights. I attempted to prod some information from him, but all he would release was that he had worked for Madame Faivre and the family of the château for a very long time. He was loyal to a fault. Any other news I wished to ascertain I would have to learn on my own during my sessions with Madame.

I know now I have come to a strange place. The chilling snow continued to fall outside and hold us prisoners, but I did not feel like a captive. Amadieu again locked the door behind me thereby keeping me bound to the space they have allocated. It might have caused some alarm if I were not so busy typing the words of Madame Faivre. Perhaps tomorrow, when she has read the work I produce, I might ask for permission to wander through the château. Being of humble means herself, surely she must know of the burning curiosity within me.

I made note to approach Madame with my request tomorrow.

14 February, mid-morning – Diary of Mademoiselle Cecilia Natashia Dupuin

Already my employer is well pleased with my craft.

This morning over breakfast I presented her with the typed pages of the words she had dictated yesterday. I stayed up well past the midnight hour studiously transcribing everything said to me. By the time it was completed, I was almost too excited to sleep. When morning finally arrived I quickly drank a warm cup of tea, refreshed myself, dressed, and almost skipped down the long spiraling staircase to where I knew Madame Faivre awaited.

Upon my arrival I noticed a look of amusement on the woman's features and wondered what tickled her so. The dear old woman only turned to her nurse and whispered something in a Germanic language, a language I had failed to learn during my studies. If Madame had been frowning, I would have profusely begged pardon, but as she seemed in good humor, I merely greeted her courteously and waited until she invited me to join her.

Just as before, a banquet fit for royalty lay before us. At her urging, I consumed the luscious dishes as she read over my transcriptions while delicately nibbling on her breakfast. Every once in a while a slight frown crossed her features, but the old matriarch waved away any concern.

"I had forgotten how painful it all was," she murmured once. I was instantly concerned, but when she saw my face she smiled and took my hand for the first time.

I know that I am naïve in matters of age and death, but

at the moment that Madame Faivre took my hand in hers, I was suddenly reminded of my purpose. Her hand held little warmth. I could feel the leather of her flesh and the sharp, angular bones below. When her fingers clasped around mine, I noticed the wince of pain that often afflicts the aged.

I have never had a mother of my own to know these feelings, nor have I ever spent time with such a woman of culture. While I sat next to her holding her hand, I saw the compassion within her dark brown eyes, and I could feel a sense of appreciation I have never felt before. In a gentle manner the bony hand clasped mine briefly before she pulled away and glanced down at the transcribed documents on her lap.

"We shall get through this," Madame Faivre said almost to herself. Before I realized a change, she turned to me, a smile softening the wrinkles in her face. "You would like to hear more, yes?"

"Yes, I would," I told her.

14 February – The recollections of Madame Agnes (Nina) Brigitte Faivre

"Those were very different times for girls. Although I lived a sheltered life, I quickly learned our value. We were vessels, like the Blessed Mother, put here on this earth for a single purpose – to procreate for the men. I never knew this before the death of my parents. When they were alive all I knew was love and kindness. My papa worked hard, and when he came home, he loved us all the more. Not an evening went by that he did not say to me, 'Nina, my shining star. One day you shall be a princess.' And I felt like one. Yes, you look at me surprised, but I truly felt like a princess to my papa. But then everything changed."

Madame Faivre grew silent as she stared into the burning flames of the fireplace.

"When my papa lay on his death bed, he asked me to look after the other children. I was to listen to Monsieur Pétain and heed his counsel. Papa said that the monsieur was his closest friend, like a brother, and that he would care for us as if we were his own." She grew silent as if remembering a pain from long ago.

"Bah! That monsieur fooled my papa like he fooled everyone else," Madame Faivre stated. "The only thing he cared for was his gold and silver, and just like Judas, his betrayal was rewarded," she assured with a knowing smile. "Yes, Monsieur Pétain fell prey to a fate that was of his own design," Madame Faivre said as a fiery expression entered her eyes. Filled with such anger, she continued to tell the tale from long ago...

*****

Inside the coach Nina found her mood matching the weather. With each droplet of rain she felt as if her soul was mourning her loss of life. To some, she may have seemed melodramatic, but she could think of nothing else. What little she knew of her betrothed led her to believe that her life, her happiness, would be gone forever. He was old, older than her papa. But he was wealthy, and with Midas on his shoulder, he was bound to make a fortune. The dowry he paid would amply pay off her papa's debts to Monsieur Pétain and hopefully, in time, she would be able to retrieve her younger siblings from the orphanage.

At the loud groaning sound next to her, Nina looked over at her fellow traveler. With his hat over his features Pétain remained comfortably nested in blankets as he slept through the turbulent journey. It was as if he did not feel the doom descending upon them. Perhaps he did not, for how could a man without a conscience ever know the turmoil of a doomed soul like hers?

Before Nina could contemplate this thought, a booming sound shook the coach. With a slight scream, she reached for the side of the coach. In an equal fashion, the Monsieur let out a loud yelp as he sat up straight. Outside she heard the neighs of the horses and the cracking of a whip before a great lurch sent them flying within the coach. Somewhere in the back of her mind she understood they were tumbling down a steep slope. She was surrounded by the horrid sounds of wailing horses and weeping men. With each jostle, she felt a pain shooting through different parts of her body until she knew no more.

When she awoke she did not know where she was. A blanket of darkness held her in its frigid grasp. Somewhere in the pitch black, she heard the sound of raging water. She felt a soft, soothing touch against her cheek. Deep in this dream state, she saw a beautiful woman kneeling by her. The woman's gentleness lessened her pain and comforted her in ways she had not felt since her own mother was alive.

In this ethereal state she heard the murmuring lullaby of a sing-song voice. "Come to me, my baby, my child. Forgive me, my love. My poor infants, what have I done?"

Before Nina could be pulled into this nightmarish dream, a thunderous sound yanked her from the warm grasp of death. She groaned as she fought her way toward consciousness. From nearby she thought she heard a multitude of whispers in the darkness. Opening her eyes she tried in vain to focus, but only saw the illusions dancing around with glee. Their shapes and forms were unknown to her, yet their whispers seemed strangely familiar. As she fought for awareness, she lifted her head and looked around.

The coach lay on its side below her, half-submerged in water as a wheel spun freakishly out of control. The horses that still lived wailed pitifully, and the heavens cried down as bolts of light flashed from above. When she heard a groan, she turned to the sound and saw the outline of Monsieur Pétain through the flash of lightning. Like her, he had been thrown from the coach, but had landed in the mud before the wooden vehicle fell upon his lower half. When he saw her, a morbid smile etched his features as a trail of blood fell past his lips.

Nina did not know what to do. She had never been trained in the healing arts. Despite this, she felt herself trying to move towards him, to offer assistance if she could. But her own pain, the ache that racked through her body brought a stifled scream from her as she fell back into the muddy embankment. The pain in her ribs, the sensations that moved from her toes to her knees were almost too much to bear. As she lay there fighting for consciousness, she glanced up at her guardian. His beseeching eyes called for her, yet she was unable to respond.

"Damn! This one is dead!" one of the fiends screamed in outrage over the sound of the storm.

The others turned to look in its direction. Dressed in the colors of night, they moved with an ungainly stride. Their elongated arms dragged upon the mud, pulling its filth in their grasp. When they saw Monsieur Pétain, low cackling screams of death roared from their bosoms. One of the fiends moved close to the injured man in a menacing manner and as the long, thin finger reached out to touch the man, a high, almost feminine cry escaped Monsieur Pétain's control.

"This one lives, we can take him," the savage beast hissed as he fondly touched the top of Monsieur Pétain's drenched hair.

From all around her, Nina heard the menacing chuckles of the unholy creatures as they circled the fallen coach. She felt her mind spinning out of control. Without a will to fight, only to live, she lay back in the mud and said a silent prayer. When she felt a deathly cold touch upon her cheek, she could not help but open her eyes to the red gaze of the devil himself.

"No, not quite." The creature seemed amused as he answered her unspoken thought. He smiled wickedly at her predicament.

"We can share her?" another beast giggled as it drew close.

"NO! Back away before I beat you!" the fiendish male voice ordered as if protecting his prized possession. "This one is special, this one is important, are you not?" it asked her, but all Nina could do was shiver.

Before she could comprehend the situation, she felt, more than saw, a sudden change in the creatures. In a subservient manner their serpent tongues hissed as they bowed and drew back from the carnage. When another flash of light flowed, Nina saw the outline of a tall form. Dressed in black with a cape flowing in the wind, the figure moved over the scene.

"My lady, I have a prize for you," the creature next to her addressed the figure.

For a moment Nina wondered if this was all a dream. She wondered if it was a delusion caused by the tumultuous fall. If she had hit her head, then perhaps she was mad, she reasoned. But if she was not gravely injured and mad, then perhaps she was dead and this was hell? Too weak to ponder the thought further, she remained motionless in the wet mud.

"I see no prize." A growl-like hiss rose from the form. "Only a wet puppy. Do with her as you please," came the decree before the figure turned and walked to Monsieur Pétain. With something akin to a growl, the tall form violently yanked the man's head back then descended upon him.

Nina felt a stifled scream lodge in her throat as she heard her guardian's shriek of pain. His arms flailed as if attempting to swat an insect, and then he grew still. Just as a flash crashed overhead the fiend turned to her with a wicked smile. Blood dripped down a monstrous chin. The creature seemed to mock her, then, as quickly as it arrived, the devil's form turned and disappeared into the cold, dark night.

"Do not mind that bit of theatrics," the monster next to her said as she felt arms reach below her and pulled her from the mud. With the sudden movement came pain, and with the pain, tears until she felt herself falling once again into oblivion. On her descent she heard the noises of the creatures.

"What shall we do with the horses?" one asked.

"Leave one for *Celle qui pleure*," the monster holding her said. "After all, it is the least we can do for the old girl."

All around her the sky opened up with a hail of flashes, but Nina did not see it. Instead she fell fitfully into the abyss of darkness. Only when at a château was she forced awake.

"Beg pardon, Mademoiselle, it is a mere formality, a custom if you will." Her lazy vision tried to focus on the voice, but found the pain in her head too great. "Now then, we welcome you into our Château. Do you enter it willingly, freely, and of your own accord?" the voice asked.

Nina stared, uncomprehending, as she fought in vain to clear the clouds within her mind. Her vision was blurry, her body ached, and the cold caused uncontrollable shivers. When she did not answer, the phantom asked the question again. This time Nina found herself shaking her head in confusion. "I-I...do not... understand." Her voice came out weak and half-alive.

"It is a very simple question, Mademoiselle. Either you accept our hospitality, or I'll have to leave you out there and let them have due course with you," the male voice stated as he turned her chin to look at the dark forest.

With no other choices before her, Nina looked at the hazy image above her. "I do," was all she said before darkness consumed her.

14 February, evening – Diary of Mademoiselle Cecilia Natashia Dupuin

I can scarcely believe what was told by Madame today. It seems impossible, improbably even, that such things could exist. Yet I cannot believe that Madame Faivre would deliberately deceive me. The descriptions of such creatures, horrid malformed demons of the dark, seem too unreal to be believed. How could such fiends come from the books to haunt the poor woman when she was in her most vulnerable state?

Perhaps her visions were simply hallucinations caused by her severe injuries. The poor woman was jostled about in such a way that it could have caused a malady of the head. The dear Madame did warn me that I might not believe her. I might even consider her to be a mad woman. Perhaps this is what she meant? But I cannot think this of her. She is no more mad than I, and whatever she experienced, whatever she believed she saw, must have occurred from her numerous injuries. I must reserve judgment until her tale is completely told. I am a student and her employee. I must fulfill my duties and chronicle her life without judgment or reservation.

I only wonder what further horrors the poor woman had to endure. I do hope it was all a nightmare. I do pray Madame Faivre only imagined such atrocities and once healed, found herself in the abode of kind, gentle souls who saved her from near death. I do pray that such evil creatures are only manifestations of an overactive imagination.

Chapter 2

15 February, morning – Diary of Mademoiselle Cecilia Natashia Dupuin

What was I to think of such a tale? All night I tossed and turned with plaguing thoughts of what my employer has told me. I tried, in vain, to convince myself it was a delusion from one badly injured, but still, the oddness of Madame Faivre's words struck home. Who was it that saved her? For what purpose did she live while her travel companions died? Most importantly what fiends existed in the woods near L'Îsère River that would have rescued her?

I can scarce ponder it all. It feels too enormous for thought, yet I cannot help myself. True, I am here to chronicle my employer's life. I must capture her words accurately and succinctly, as I was taught at Madame Ségolène's school. Yet while I learned every form of scribing and the rudiments of form, there was nothing mentioned to help me not ponder more than needed. How am I expected to chronicle the tales of Madame Faivre and not feel the pain of her life?

Yet I must. My task, my duty is to transcribe her words verbatim, and this I shall do.

15 February – The recollections of Madame Agnes (Nina) Brigitte Faivre

"Come, child. Come and sit with me so that we may dine. Please, do not let my tale of yesterday affect your youthful appetite." Madame Faivre's voice was soft and soothing. "Eat, enjoy the plenty that I have been blessed with and I shall recollect more of that time, if I am able."

I could not help but point out to my employer the necessity of needing a free hand to transcribe. Were it not for the grumbling of my stomach, I might have begun without partaking of breakfast. Thankfully, Madame Faivre realized my situation and merely gave me a knowing smile as she responded, "What is that you say? Well of course, of course. An excellent transcriber such as yourself shall require a free hand. That is true, so true. How odd that I should not think of that. You know, once my mind was excellent. I could remember everything in great detail. But now, alas, age is toying with me greatly. So we shall dine, then we shall begin a new day, yes?" She smiled as she passed a tray of warm biscuits to me and we dined over trifling conversations.

"Very well, with breakfast out of the way we shall begin a new day, a new chronicle of this old lady," Madame Faivre said, and I tried to wash away her comments with a compliment.

She looked at me confused and said, "What?"

"Madame, you are hardly old," I stated again.

When she understood my compliment, a modest smile crossed her withered features. "But you flatter me, child. Yes you truly do. If you knew how truly old I am. But that is for another day, I fear. For now, we must begin our daily task."

"By now you must be asking yourself if what I saw that night of the accident was real, or the result of damage to my brain. Trust me, I asked myself that very same question. Day after day, night after tremulous night, I wondered the exact thing because you see, I was ill for a very long time. Thankfully, I had a good nurse, with hands that healed me and brought me back to myself. But that comes later. Right now I should like to explain, as best as possible, what happened after the accident. Perhaps then you shall understand further what transpired after that fateful night," she said as she began her tale from long ago...

*****

The howling winds raged outside the château, but Nina did not notice. Her savior, a fiend only imagined in the darkest of nightmares, had placed her in the comfort of a soft, warm bed. A few times she awoke to find herself dressed in a nightgown, her wounds covered with ointment and bandaged. Initially she could do nothing but peacefully fall back into slumber, but gradually, as the ache of her body raged, she began to move.

A slight tsking sound came from somewhere in the darkness, "Not yet, *Poupette*, not yet," a distinctly male voice ordered as Nina rose from the pit of her agony. At the urging, she remained in a prone position and no longer attempted to rise. When she managed to open her eyes, she saw a smiling face looking down at her. The hideous beast of her memories was replaced by a young, dark haired man. She could not place his age, but guessed he was not much older than her. He appeared to be in his twenties, yet his mannerisms seemed far more mature. His dark hair hung past his shoulders and his neatly trimmed goatee brought an elegant appearance to his lean form. Smiling down at her, she noticed the oddity of his two sharp canine teeth, but before her mind could make sense of it, he leaned toward her and pulled the coverlet over her shoulders.

"Perhaps tomorrow, *Poupette*, you will be able to venture from your sick bed. Until then, you must rest and let you Amadieu tend to your every needs." The young man gave her a toothy smile.

Nina tried, in vain, to move her parched lips. As if reading her mind, Amadieu moved to the side of the bed and poured water into a crystal goblet. Like a mother with a babe, he gently lifted her and held the vessel to her lips. With a slight cooing sound, Amadieu encouraged her to drink and then slowly withdrew the goblet from her lips.

"Enough, Nina. It has been days. You do not wish to become ill by drinking too much too soon. In time, you will be restored," her new caretaker assured as he returned the goblet to the table by the bed.

"H-How do you know my name?" Nina's voice came out soft and raspy, the pain of disuse evident.

"Why, you told me." The young stranger smiled down at her. "As for where you are, you are at the château of Lady de la Fontaine. You are her guest, and I am your," he hesitated. With a devilish smile, he gazed down at the injured girl. "I am you savior, your humble servant, and protector." A bemused smile crossed his face.

By the light of the candle, she noticed a sparkle glimmer off of his teeth and for a moment, her mind recoiled at the memory of the red-eyed devil looking down at her by the river. But the image quickly vanished when he lightly stroked her forehead.

"Now sleep, *Poupette*. Sleep and dream of healing," Amadieu's hypnotic voice soothed her troubling thoughts. She found her eyes drooping as she was lulled back into a deep slumber.

In her dreams Nina relived the accident over and over again. She felt herself tumbling in the air, felt the cold rain soaking her to the bones, and heard the sounds of hushed voices all around her. The recurring nightmares were of a mystical land unknown to her. In her fantasy world she found herself walking in a dark mist. Although she did not see anything in the pitch black, she could hear the soft murmurs of voices like a hive of bees. Once or twice, she called out, but found herself alone. Just when the sensations of abandonment would consume her, she felt another, a spirit, an entity – something, close by, beckoning her nearer. But each time she came close to the phantom, she found herself shaken awake with fear. Sometimes Amadieu was there to soothe her fears, but many times she was alone in the memories of her dreams.

When Nina first arrived she could not tell night from day because in her delicate and frail condition time was endless. She was not even aware that another birthday had come and gone, so she celebrated her seventeenth birthday alone and blissfully ignorant of time. The cycles of her caretaker, Amadieu, were like the strike of a clock. At various intervals he checked on her, tended to her, and despite whatever modesty might have afflicted her in the past, she was void of them now. As her health returned, she began to relish his companionship.

Nina excelled in self-awareness. Just as she became gradually aware of her circumstances, she began to notice everything around her. While confined in the bed to heal, she noticed the golden cloth hung around her bed like a curtain. Whenever Amadieu entered her quarters, she heard the soft clicking of his heels on the marble corridor outside her chamber. Once or twice, she tried to move from her bed but found her strength lacking. Rather than attempting it too early, she allowed her caretaker, and only friend, to revive her back to health.

"Who is the lady of the house?" Nina once asked of her friend.

The spoon of soup stopped in midair as Amadieu examined her closely and appeared to be debating with himself. His brows creased in thought as the spoon he held remained above the bowl. The smile usually on his lips vanished, and his lips grew thin in between his goatee. Then it seemed as if he nodded to himself before looking her straight in the eyes. As if resolved, he smiled as he continued to feed her.

"She is just a lady like any other," he said before spooning the warm broth for her.

"Why have I not seen her?" Nina asked, her nonstop questions not fazing the young man.

"She will be seen when she wants to be seen. Now stop worrying over questions and eat. You'll be well in time, and then you may have the answer that you desire." Amadieu smiled softly.

Yet despite Amadieu's promise, Nina found the answer to her questions elusive. Confined to bed, still weak from the trauma, all she could do was lay and rest while her mind continued to churn over a multitude of questions. Once or twice, she wondered if Monsieur Pétain was similarly resting within the château. She wondered if he was also recuperating in a nearby room. But each time she wondered about it, a pounding in her head began until all she could do was close her eyes to sleep in hope it would vanish.

On a day when the winds stopped pelting the rain against the barred window and the cold chill of gently falling snow could be felt in the room, she found herself staring at the ornate canopy above her. When she leaned over and slightly parted curtains, she noticed the diffused sunlight escaping through the tight wooden shutters of the windows. Nina knew it was daytime because of the sun streaming in through the shutters. At night the temperature dropped and, on most nights, Amadieu was with her. She was healing enough to become aware of the cycles around her. She would not see Amadieu again until darkness fell over the château. Nina did not know why her new friend kept these hours but assumed it had to do with his duties.

Now that she was more aware of her surroundings, Nina found herself longing to venture from her bed. *If I can walk without feeling faint, then perhaps I can venture into the rest of the château,* she thought as she lay silent under the thick covers.

From somewhere in the room she heard a slight scratching. It was like the sound of rats upon a tiled room. When she listened more closely, she heard it periodically in the room. As she strained to ascertain its origin, she became aware of the slight crackling of wood in the fireplace, its leaping flames heating the large room. If there was movement in the château, she did not hear it. Perhaps they were quiet people, or she was located too far back in the home to be near the foot traffic.

Again, the sound of rat claws scratched nearby. At the curious noise, Nina sat up and slowly parted the bed curtain. Almost afraid of what she would find, she peered out and glanced at the shadows in her room. Near silence greet her. The interminable silence was interrupted by the familiar scratching. Nina cautiously moved her hand to the single candle by her bed. Careful of her condition, she slowly rose from the bed and lifted the candle in hand. Although she had walked a few steps with Amadieu, she had never ventured alone. Now, she took her first tentative step. She felt dizzy, and the pain of disuse in her legs caused her to wobble. Despite the discomfort she ventured further into her room.

From somewhere nearby she heard the soft scratching sounds again. Nina held the candle high and glanced around the room. She noticed the armoire in the corner. The slight sunlight from outside showed the intricate designs in the wood. Nearby was a dressing table covered with bottles of perfume from Paris. At the farthest corner of the room, wood crackled in the large fireplace. Standing in the center of the room and wearing a nightdress, she searched for the sound of scratching. As if reading her mind, the sound came again from above her head.

Nina did not know why, but her heart suddenly beat in fearful anticipation. With her long dark hair spilling past her shoulders, she slowly turned her gaze upward to the ceiling. Her eyes grew wide in horror as she saw the form of a hideous monster. Its body was as large as a man, its flesh had scales like a reptile and arms, if arms they be, were curled around its torso like bat wings. Long, thin legs gave way to clawed feet and nails, longer than any talons she had ever imagined, dug deeply into the ceiling. Suddenly the monstrous creature opened its beady red eyes. The reptilian nose sniffed the air, then the beast looked down at her. Nina screamed, then swooned, falling in a heap. The candle dropped heedlessly by her feet.

When Nina awoke, she was back in her bed with the blankets drawn over her. Amadieu sat holding her hand. In fear and despair she sat bolt upright in bed. Her eyes glazed over as she glanced fearfully around the room. "Amadieu, oh Amadieu, there was a beast in here, a hideous creature that," she began to say but was quieted by the man's gentle touch.

"No, no, no, sweet one. Calm yourself. Do not unduly upset yourself. There is nothing in this room for you to fear," Amadieu assured.

"Are you," she hesitated and looked at him with pleading eyes, "certain?"

"I am positive." He smiled. "I've been with you the entire time, and let me assure you, there is absolutely nothing to fear in this room. You are safe. Trust your Amadieu." The man's assuring words calmed her spirit.

"Oh Amadieu, it was hideous." Nina closed her eyes to the memory of the apparition that she beheld.

"Nonsense, calm yourself. It was only a dream, just a dream," Amadieu cooed. "You should not be venturing out of bed so soon. Why, it is no wonder that you hallucinated with your weakened state. Calm yourself, child. Rest and listen to your Amadieu. In no time at all your strength will be restored and you will be able to venture out by yourself," he stated.

"Venture out?" She looked at him surprised.

"What? You think I keep you a prisoner?" Amadieu's voice shooed away her thoughts with a feminine wave of his hand. "Silly child, as soon as you are well, you may venture out unassisted. But for now, it is important for you to rest and heal yourself," he said.

Nina took his word to heart. When she thought of it, she found herself agreeing with her new friend. Amadieu was right. She was still weak, still healing. In such a state it was no wonder she would envision such monstrous hallucinations, she told herself, determined to focus all of her energies upon her health.

15 February, evening – Diary of Mademoiselle Cecilia Natashia Dupuin

It is no wonder the poor dear doubts her own memories? The injuries, damage to her body, surely affected her spirits. Now, in her golden years, she finds herself filled with the nightmare of her past. I can only hope her tale grows brighter. Madame Faivre is such a wonderful person; I only wish for her happiness. If her life is filled with memories of trauma, what happiness could she have found?

But enough of these musings. As soon as our session was over, she bid me to dine with her. Once freshened and changed into my good dress, I joined Madame Faivre for a sumptuous meal served in the dining room. It was not the great hall where lavish parties were once thrown but a smaller room which housed an intimate setting. I had hoped to meet the mistress of the house, Lady de la Fontaine, but was told she seldom dined with guests anymore.

As we supped together I wondered if the mistress was as infirmed as Madame Faivre. I wondered if, like my employer, the Lady was near the ending stage of her life. Perhaps she was bedridden and unable to venture from her room?

So many questions arose with so few answers. Rather than learn more over dinner, I was questioned by Madame Faivre about the numerous events of Paris. As I was only a student of Madame Ségolène's school for girls, I could aptly impart all the news of this little establishment but hardly anything of the politics of the city. Important plays, dramas, or even social events seemed lost to me. However, this did not appear to affect Madame Faivre, and she listened to my gossip of the school with avid interest.

Either my dinner conversation warranted a reward, or perhaps she was pleased with my job, but as soon as dinner ended, Madame Faivre asked me to join her. For the first time I was escorted through the first floor of the château. With her faithful nurse pushing her wheelchair, I followed alongside. I listened with rapt attention to her monologue and was intrigued by the numerous paintings hung on the stone walls. With all of the candles lighting the way, I noticed many different artists whose skillful hands had created these masterpieces. Seemingly pleased by my attention, Madame Faivre gave a complete account of the history behind each work.

Before I realized the change we entered a larger room. Anticipating his mistress' needs, Frederic stood in the smaller room. The lanterns were lit and cast a bright glow upon every wall. When I walked in, my eyes grew wide with amazement as I gazed lovingly at the tall shelves covering the walls from floor to ceiling, all filled with an endless array of books.

"Ah, I see your appreciation is similar to my own." Madame Faivre smiled as she was wheeled further into the library. "I am afraid, my dear, that I have neglected to show you this treasured area of the château. Please, Mademoiselle Dupuin, take leave of any book within our collection," she said as she smiled up to Frederic.

"And what, Frederic, shall amuse me tonight before I drift off to slumber?" Madame Faivre asked the tall man.

"I thought perhaps a bit of Warpole, Madame," he answered his mistress formally as he handed her a leather-bound book.

"Ahhh, *The Castle of Otranto*." Madame Faivre smiled as her shaky hand took the book. "I do like a bit of decadence every now and again." She winked at me as she placed the book in her lap. "And as for you, my dear," she turned to Frederic for another book. With a slight bow, he handed her another leather-bound novel. "How about a bit of adventure, yes?" She handed me the book.

I looked at the volume and smiled from ear to ear. *How did she know that* The Arabian Nights *was my favorite?* I wondered.

As if clairvoyant, she answered my unspoken question. "A...little bird suggested that this might be your favorite reading." Madame Faivre smiled warmly, then turned and waved to her nurse. "Please feel free to take however many you might wish to your quarters. Frederic will escort you to your room when you have chosen." The nurse wheeled Madame Faivre from the room.

As she was taken down the long corridor, Madame Faivre's voice echoed from the walls. "Allow your mind to consume the words and take you elsewhere. Trust me, child, it will help you in the future endeavors that face us in the coming days." Her words were lost on me as I moved to examine the enormous collection of books.

I could have stayed there all night, and surely I must have been there a good time. As the silence wore on I did not wish to appear greedy, so rather than take more books that beckoned me, I left the library with the single book that Madame Faivre guessed correctly was my favorite tale of all. Frederic said nothing but smiled as he escorted me through the labyrinth of hallways until I was at the bottom of the spiraling staircase.

"Amadieu is waiting for you," was all Frederic said as I gingerly skipped up the steps to my room. With the book in hand, it did not even occur to me to question the purpose for my room to be locked every night. The comfort and warmth received from Madame Faivre put me at ease, and now with a book, I knew that I could take some leisure time and fall into slumber with any number of tales, rather than allowing my suspicious mind to ponder this wonderful château.

16 February – The recollections of Madame Agnes (Nina) Brigitte Faivre

"So, you have stayed up late reading, yes? Oh, do not try to hide the yawn. I myself was up late." Madame Faivre's accusatory words held mirth. "But then, the elderly tend not to need as much sleep, do we?" Come, come and sit and share this wonderful breakfast. It is not often that we have such delicacies during the winter. But this year is special. This year is different, and every day shall be like a holiday where a feast will be set for all to enjoy," she proclaimed with glee.

With idle chatter we passed the morning until the servants removed the plates. Then we moved, as was customary, to the study for our day of transcribing.

"Now then, where did we last leave off? Yes, yes, my healing after the terrible accident. What a hard time that was, too. It took all winter before I could even venture to walk alone in my room. Of course by that time I realized that whatever I saw, whatever phantom might have been in the room with me on that day, was not a phantom at all. But then, that is usually how it turns out, do you not agree? The unknown is oftentimes frightening. However, in due course, when light is shed upon the shadows, we discover that our fears played a great part of our perceptions," Madame Faivre cryptically stated.

"But enough of my ramblings, we shall continue," she said, her eyes growing distant and her voice soft as she continued to tale...

*****

By the time the blizzard ended and the crisp snow slowly gave way to the beginning of spring, Nina finally found herself recuperated. She could walk through her large room without assistance and began to take care of herself, but she had yet to venture outside of her room. After so many months of his gentle assistance, she trusted Amadieu completely. Sometimes Nina wanted to liken him to a brother, but other times, when she contemplated all he did for her, she realized that he was closer than a brother. Yet there was no romantic love involved; this she knew for certain.

Although he never stated it, Nina understood the young servant's interest were not toward her. With his gentle nature and feminine gait, she was fully aware that his proclivities did not lay with her gender. Manners like this, dandies like this, were seldom seen, and she had only heard of them in passing. Such men were whispered about, some even mocked. If rumors were true, many resided in the town of Paris.

Amadieu had been to Paris with his mistress. Many nights on end he retold his tales of the bright city. With an almost wicked smile, he informed her of the gay Parisians that he had met through his journeys. Other times he whispered of the abandoned joy he received from one such gent or another. He was never explicit with her, but his low, melodic voice conveyed images far more graphic than could words by themselves.

Nina enjoyed these evenings with her friend. Now that she could move around on her own, she began to cherish him as a friend rather than a nursemaid. Amadieu seemed equally pleased with her company. Like naughty schoolgirls, they stayed up well past the witching hour to talk and giggle as they exchanged stories of their antics.

On one particular night, when the château was at its quietest, Nina released a tired sigh. "Amadieu, I'm bored," she proclaimed as the winter frost was melting into a steady stream toward the L'Îsère River.

"Oh no, I know exactly what is happening." The tall man shook his head. He reclined on her large bed, a file in hand as he groomed his nails.

Nina stood at the open window of her room on the second floor. With winter gone the shutters were removed and only the curtains remained to keep the cold chill at bay. Soon, spring would be in full force and they could leave the windows open for the scent of spring flowers to freshen the room.

"Amadieu, why is there only silence in the daytime? Where are the people of the château?" Nina asked as she folded her arms in front of her.

"I told you, *Poupette*, the mistress is a very busy woman. It is only her and us servants. She seldom frequents the place, let alone is here in the daytime. After all, she does all of her work at night, as do the rest of us," he said.

"And you? Where are you in the daytime?" She turned to face him with a slight frown on her face.

"I, young lady, am tending to whatever chores I didn't get to while I am here with you." Amadieu smiled as he rose from the bed and moved to stand before her. "I know you're feeling restless. It's only natural. I only ask that you have more patience, please. For my sake." He smiled as he gently took her chin in hand. "Do I not bring you endless books to read from the library? Are there not enough tales to keep you occupied for many seasons to come?" he asked.

"Yes, but," Nina stammered as she turned away from him, the warmth of embarrassment crossing her cheeks. "Who is the lady of the house? What does she do that she only moves about by night? Where does she go in the daytime? Is she really so queer, or does she have a rare skin ailment, something that precludes her venturing into the sunlight?" Her questions rolled freely from her tongue.

The tall man began to laugh as he waved away her rapid fire questions. "I have told you who the lady of the house is, and yes, she only moves about at night. If it helps you to understand, then think of it as a medical ailment. But trust me, she is here. She does reside in the château. Promise me, Poupette, do not venture out yet. I give my solemn word, in due course you can leave your room, and I will show you the entire château. Then, hopefully, you'll meet Lady de la Fontaine personally," Amadieu said.

At first Nina pouted like someone much younger. Then as she saw the intensity of Amadieu's gaze, she found her resolve slowly crumbling. With a slight smile, she nodded assent. "I promise, I will wait," she capitulated. "But I do not promise to like it," she added which caused a soft laugh to escape the man's control.

"I would expect nothing less," Amadieu said as he pulled her into his cold embrace.

Sometimes promises were easy to keep. Promising to take care of a loved one, to look after a child, or attend to your studies. But there were other promises not as easily kept, like staying indoors when the cold winter breeze slowly changed into spring. Now that the chilling winter winds were behind them, the windows in her room remained open for the day. The drapes were pulled back, and the sun filtered into her quarters with abandon. Whatever monsters resided in the darkness were not vanquished with the coming spring.

With a slight frown, Nina leaned on an elbow as she gazed out of her bedroom window. She noticed the lush grass which once lay dormant below a deep blanket of snow. In the distant forest she watched the birds flying over the trees. When she concentrated fully she could almost hear the rushing currents of L'Îsère River. *The newly melted snow surely brought the level of the water up,* she silently thought as she released a sigh.

Nina turned her glance to her room and looked at every object. After such a long time healing, every item was etched in her memory. The opulent furniture, the scenic oil canvas on the wall, even the designs in the marble floor had been committed to memory. She felt she knew every inch of this room, and it bored her to even contemplate this.

When Nina moved to the nearby table she absently gazed at the piles of books her friend had brought. Her delicate fingers traced the familiar titles. There was a time when these words were her refuge and comfort in the cold winter days. While she was healing, Amadieu read the tales to her aloud, complete with flamboyant gestures and theatrics. When she was well enough to occupy herself, she alternated her days by reading these books and napping until her friend joined her at night. Now, as she glanced at them, a tired sigh escaped her control.

It was spring and Nina was young and bored.

Should she be caught by the lady of the house, she would beg the mistress to remember the days when she, herself, was a young girl and spring was in the air. Despite everything urging restraint, Nina moved deliberately toward the single door. Once at the door she hesitated, her palm resting on the thick, hard wood. Her hand trembled as it moved to the golden doorknob. Then, without much ado, she pulled on the knob and was surprised to hear the slight sound of squeaking hinges breaking through the silence.

Her heart beating uncontrollably, Nina stood on the threshold of her room. Outside, the corridor was filled with shadows, but the pale light of the sun glimmered in through the partially curtained windows. Cautiously she leaned forward and peered out, almost expecting to have her head chopped off by a guardian spirit. When nothing happened, she took a tentative step forward.

Nothing was as innate as the fight against tyranny and the

longing for freedom. Just like many of her countrymen, Nina cherished her freedom, and like them, she took the glorious steps needed to attain true happiness. While a part of her longed to explore the château, another part wanted to bathe in the sunlight. With nothing else in mind she made her way down the long corridor. Instinctively, she found her way to the staircase until she reached the open foyer. With only a single glance back, she yanked open the door.

Of all the experiences she had encountered, Nina found this one to be the most pleasant. She wore the borrowed dress that Amadieu gave her. It was simple in design and of ordinary fabric with a low-cut bodice and short sleeves. Upon taking her first steps into the sunlight, she felt its warmth crawling up her flesh. With a smile she moved further into the spring day.

Walking out onto the open grass, a part of Nina felt guilty. She should have been worried about her siblings, but Amadieu promised that he was searching for them. Although she loathed the man, a part of her soul felt it improper to not mourn Monsieur Pétain's passing. Amadieu never told her how the man died, only vaguely explaining that night. Although her memories were like a fleeting nightmare, she knew Amadieu spoke the truth when he said that she was the sole survivor. For all of this, Nina felt guilty, and part of her felt it disrespectful to find such pleasure in the spring morning. Yet there was another part unable to resist the temptation. So with all of her youthful exuberance, she left the confines of the château.

In the early morning sunlight, Nina walked over the open grass as far as the edge of the forest. She inhaled the sweet scent of spring. When she heard the birds chirping, she glanced up, shielding her eyes against the sunlight. A smile curled her lips as she watched the delicate creatures soaring through the air. Within their beaks they carried the various twigs needed to build nests for the coming hatchlings.

When she turned back, Nina examined the outline of the château for the first time. It was an ominous creature crouching in the shadows at the edge of the forest. Behind it, the tall, jagged teeth of the French Alps strained upward toward the heavens. Before it stretched an open, grassy area filled with spring flowers and the fresh scent of dew.

The château was three stories tall with round turrets rising another story at each corner. The turrets were steepled while the rest of the roof remained flat. At the corners, gargoyles sneered down, watching everything with their stony gaze. Nina kept turning her head to study the grotesque statues more carefully, thinking they had turned to watch her. "But that is silly," she told herself. It was just the dancing shadows playing tricks at the edge of her vision.

Nina regarded the building once more. Its sheer size made her wonder how many generations went into building such grandeur. She was certain this one was not as elegant as the chateaus of Paris, but to her, it was the largest mansion she had ever seen. Many of its windows remained closed up from the sun. Only hers was open. As she gazed at the structure she marveled at the craftsmanship which had gone into its building.

She was not in a hurry to return to the familiar walls of her convalescence. So rather than making her way directly, she walked aimlessly through the tall green grass. Occasionally she knelt down to pick wild flowers. She made her way to the château once she had a full bouquet. Rather than entering the front door, she explored the exterior of the building. After a short walk she discovered the château's garden. With great effort, Nina entered through the lopsided gate. Where there should have been a variety of flowers and trees sat the rubble which comes from years of neglect. Moving further along the outside, she found herself in what must be the family cemetery. Its dilapidation mirrored the garden.

Nina was not a superstitious woman, but as she walked through the cemetery she felt her heart aching for the long forgotten souls buried here. The marble statues, once mighty centurions guarding the remains of the dead, were falling apart or barely held together against the ravages of time. Where there was lush green grass growing freely in the open meadow at the front of the château, the cemetery was covered with broken tiles, weeds and briars. Moving deeper into the solitude, Nina glanced at the names on the tombstones and whispered a silent prayer. Only when she came to a pristine section did she stop to examine the area in detail.

Here lay a circular area with large marble statues of angels flanking the edge. In the center of the area stood a structure resembling a mausoleum. Instead of the familiar arched roof, the top was flat and held another sculpture. When Nina walked closer, she noticed that the crypt was made of rich, highly-polished white marble. The elaborate design of the wrought iron door gave testament to the skill of some unknown master artisan.

Looking up, Nina was able to closely inspect the statue on the roof of the mausoleum. Poised above the crypt, the colossal angel took her breath away. With its face hidden and its wings folded gently, it sprawled over a marble platform, a single arm extended forward and laying limp as if in grief. Although the features were hidden, its body position clearly conveyed the feelings of utter grief and despair. Nina felt her breath taken away by such hopelessness.

Her gaze fell to the area around the crypt. In contrast to the rest of the cemetery, this area was well maintained with a manicured lawn and nothing out of place. The angel statues that circled the crypt were in perfect condition without scratches or discoloration. At the foot of the iron gate sat a polished marble marker.

When Nina's eyes beheld this, a deep sorrow entered her soul. Lying upon the marble was a fresh bouquet of flowers very much like the one in her hand. As she knelt down, she glanced back up at the statue and felt the pain and love that must have gone into the crypt. Filled with respectful reverence, she lifted the flowers and read the inscription on the marker.

Isabelle, Baronne De La Chorange 1778 – 1818

16 February, evening – Diary of Mademoiselle Cecilia Natashia Dupuin

A great sorrow fills my heart as I transcribe today's session. Although Madame Faivre did not say it, I could tell by her words how her heart lamented at this find. Here I sit in tears over such sorrow, yet I cannot explain why. This château is filled with mysteries and sadness, this much is true. With each passing day I find myself enthralled by the tales of my employer and find myself wondering if this is simply an elaborate fable. But as I contemplate this, I scold myself. Madame Faivre is a kind and generous woman. She has never led me astray, and although she continues to state she had unremarkable beginnings, I cannot help but see how extraordinary her life truly is.

No amount of prodding Amadieu would get him to reveal anything new. When I questioned if he was named after an ancestor who once worked for Madame Faivre, all he would do is smile and reply, "You could think of it that way."

Surely he must know the secrets of the château, having lived here for many generations with his own parents and grand-parents, however he revealed nothing. For the answers I must wait, but waiting is becoming increasingly difficult.

Thank goodness I have literature to keep me occupied, lest I find myself going mad with wanting to know the whole truth. In due course, I am told. The entire tale will be revealed to me in due course.

Chapter 3

**17 February, morning – Diary of Mademoiselle Cecilia
Natashia Dupuin**

I find my task more intriguing with each passing day. I received word this morning from Frederic that Madame Faivre had begged my pardon. At first I was greatly worried, but was assured by the servant that it was merely fatigue. This happens often for the elderly, and I am certain he is correct. Hopefully she will be well soon, and we can resume her transcription. I do so wish to learn more about her and this grand château.

On a positive note, I have been allowed to wander through the first floors. With Frederic at my side, I was shown a great deal more of the home besides the library. What a stark difference it must have been from Madame Faivre's first venture through the home. If her memories are correct, which I dearly hope are a combination of truth and fancy, the château was dark and abandoned. As Frederic conducted the tour, he pointed out the various works of art, their origin, and named the artists. For titillation, he whispered the various scandals regarding each artist.

As I walked along the brightly lit corridors and marveled at the decorations, I found it hard to imagine the place in shadows. The maids walked to and fro about their business. Each one smiled and issued forth a greeting as only one servant could do to another. All around me was the low murmur of voices and people moving about. There appeared to be a great number of staff on hand to keep such a large establishment running smoothly and I wondered what had happened those many years ago when Madame Faivre found the place so empty.

I find it difficult to imagine such a grand palace as dark, cold and void of life, especially after I see such movement within it. Perhaps in time I shall learn the cause of such condition.

18 February, morning – Diary of Mademoiselle Cecilia Natashia Dupuin

Madame Faivre took leave to travel to Geneva. I do not know what it was about, but early morning before the dawn I heard a commotion from below my window. Quickly I rose and with only my nightdress, I parted the curtains and gazed down upon the most amazing sight.

I watched below me as Amadieu held open a carriage door. A taller figure, one who I had never met, left the château carrying the bundled form of Madame Faivre. This stranger was dressed in an elegant black coat, neatly pressed trousers and black leather gloves. Although I could not see clearly through the night and dim candle light from below, I could almost imagine this stranger wearing a fine suit of the grandest nature. His long black hair flowed freely in the wind. The figure was so gentle that I could not help but wonder if this was her husband, or perhaps her son? The figure, so tall and lean, moved with such youthful grace that I could not imagine him to be Madame Faivre's husband. Unless...no, this is wicked of me to think this. Perhaps she married a much younger man? If so, this leads to more questions to ponder.

Is the young upstart using poor Madame Faivre? Could he think that by using this ruse he would inherit her wealth? No, I cannot think like this for it already raises my ire. I hardly know her, yet already I am overprotective of my employer.

So Madame Faivre, through a message delivered by Frederic this morning, begged leave of me for a short duration. She is traveling to Geneva for her health. Thankfully the Swiss border is but a short distance away. Ever-faithful, Amadieu has traveled with her and the strange companion. Until she returns I have been given leave to do as I will, and now with my newfound freedom I am not all together certain where to begin.

24 February, evening – Diary of Mademoiselle Cecilia Natashia Dupuin

Already it has been a week, and I have exhausted my exploration of the château. I saw the gardens, Madame Faivre's pride and joy, covered with a blanket of snow. Yet, I could see the gentle care taken with everything in her domain. In an area of the garden was a new structure built to remain warm in the winter. Within it the grounds keepers tended the seedlings to be placed in the gardens and around the château come spring. Each man greeted me courteously but continued with their duties. Not wishing to disturb their work, I left them in peace.

It is a queer thing to see the cemetery that Madame Faivre mentioned in her last transcription. Many of the statues were still in the ruin, but a great deal has been restored. Although I do admit it is difficult to judge owing to the snow covering the ground. Even so it felt as if there was a resurrection of life in this dwelling of death.

As I moved further into the area, I noticed the crypt my employer had also mentioned. Snow covered the immaculate angel forever in mourning. When I moved to the front gated door, I noticed the same marble marker. It was covered by snow and instead of flowers, which surely would not have survived, there sat a beautiful rose cast out of bronze and permanently affixed.

"Who are you, Isabelle, Baronne De La Chorange?" What mystery must you hold," I wondered aloud as I gazed solemnly upon the marker. Yet I knew that I would receive no answers on this day.

27 February, morning – Diary of Mademoiselle Cecilia Natashia Dupuin

I have found the chapel in the château. It is a small place, large enough for only a handful. While the château itself appears older, this chapel seems to have been built in the past few decades. From what I remember of my art studies at Madame Ségolène's school, the mosaic ceiling depicting Lazarus rising from the dead, is modern. Both the Christ figure and Holy Virgin statues standing in the front are current designs. The stained glass windows lining all sides of the chapel hold images of valiant saints.

I do not know why but I find myself reverting back to the time of my days at the orphanage. I found my rosary, and I have taken to visiting the chapel every morning and night. I never thought I would ever revert back to old superstitions. I am an educated woman, a modern woman. I studied the arts and science and know that much of what the sisters taught are mere superstitions. But I still cannot help but go through the litany. I cannot help but send up a silent prayer for the health and safety of my employer, Madame Faivre. I hope that her health is good. I hope that the clinic in Geneva will heal what ails the poor woman.

Surely it cannot hurt to hold such wishes? And if there be a God to listen, perhaps He will have mercy and spare the grand lady any further pain?

29 February, morning – Diary of Mademoiselle Cecilia Natashia Dupuin

Madame Faivre returned just as she left. I awoke to hear the carriage this morning. When I ran to the window, I looked down and beheld the same sight. Amadieu was already out of the carriage when someone from within handed him the bundle of my employer. She was wrapped tightly like a baby, but even from the second floor I could hear her gentle banter. The servant held her closely, and when a taller figure emerged, Amadieu turned the grand dame over to him.

Dressed all in black and by the dimness of light I could not, once again, discern the identity of this figure. Not even the single lamp held by the head maid who stood at the archway helped me see the mysterious man who carried my employer into the home.

I am very pleased that she is well again. Soon, I hope to hear all of the news from her.

1 March, morning – Diary of Mademoiselle Cecilia Natashia Dupuin

Madame Faivre is such a wonderful woman. Even when she was laying ill in the clinic at Geneva, she stated she thought of me. She told me all she had seen, omitting the medical procedures she endured, and talked a great deal about the city. As she was recuperating she sent her companion, yes, that is what she called him, her companion to purchase some trinkets for me. There were new clothes, dresses, undergarments which I blush to consider a man purchasing, coats and shawls. I feigned to dear Madame Faivre I did not have need for such glamorous gifts. She refused my words and insisted I make her happy by accepting them, at which I gratefully complied.

In addition to the clothing she had a special music box which she stated struck her fancy and knew that I, too, would enjoy it. It is the most beautiful item I have ever owned. The box has inlaid designs of birds and flowers and holds a fine sheen. Upon opening, the sound of Pachelbel's Canon in D floated through the air with such grace. When I heard the beautiful music I could only shed tears at the sheer beauty of it.

Madame Faivre was at once concerned but I assured her that they were tears of happiness, nothing more. She was well pleased.

In a few days, once she rests from the journey, we shall begin transcriptions again.

4 March – The recollections of Madame Agnes (Nina) Brigitte Faivre

"So I hear that you have made use of the château?" Madame Faivre asked.

I grew immediately concerned, "I beg pardon if I offended, Madame."

"Oh, do not grow concerned, child. I gave you leave to explore, and I am sure you must admit your way of exploring is far more preferable to mine." She smiled as she patted my hand fondly. "Yes, the old place looks vastly different in the daylight with the curtain opened to let what little sun there is in. How drastically different it all is when the lamps are lit and the servants are about." Madame Faivre's eyes grew distant, as if returning to a different place and time.

"But I prattle on too much, yes? Come now, let us begin where we left off." She shook herself out of her silent reflections.

"Back then I was much like you are now. Young, precocious, and filled with an insatiable curiosity to learn all that there is to know of life. I was curious about everything, especially about this château. But back then, the answers I longed for were not forthcoming as they are now to you. Hopefully in time, you will understand everything and will not fault this poor old woman for the manner in expression, which brought forth my own assurances.

"I could never find fault or be angry with you, Madame. You have been so kind to me, and I gladly transcribe your words," I stated with conviction.

"What is that you say? Oh, you are dear to say so. Yes, you say now that you could never fault me, could never be angry with me, but I wonder. Well, we might never know. Come, let us begin our work, and I will tell you more of my early life in this château," she said as her expression grew reflective. She spoke of those days from long ago...

*****

"Nina, you cannot venture out of this room alone!" Amadieu's anger rose audibly.

"Why not, Amadieu?" She stomped her foot like a petulant child before crossing her arms in front of her as her brows creased and her lips turned downward into a frown. "I am well again. I can walk on my own, and I'm tired of staying in this room day in and day out. I want to see what lies beyond these doors."

Amadieu gave a tired sigh. "*Poupette.*" He shook his head as he began pacing the length of the room. When she saw him pacing, she grew calm and moved to sit on the divan as she waited for his reply.

All of the lamps were lit in her room to give an air of daylight. As she sat on the large divan she glanced around her room. The telltale evidence of her exploits sat on the table. The flowers, neatly arranged, sat within her water glass. If it had not been for this evidence of spring, her guardian, and new friend, might never have known she had wandered out alone in the daytime.

Now, as he gazed at the flowers, she paced nervously to and fro. "Ah, *Poupette*, what am I to do with you?" he moaned.

"Why can I not leave, Amadieu? There is no one here; it is empty," Nina stated with a bit of anger as she rose to stand by the warm embers in the fireplace.

"Oh, if you only knew, little one. If you only knew of the circumstances," the tall man said in a whisper as he looked at her deeply. For a moment she thought that he would at last reveal something, perhaps tall her where the people were within the château, but then he shook his head in anger and turned away from her.

"Tell me, Amadieu. Are we not friends? Have you not stated many times that you are friend to me?" Nina moved to him and lightly placed her hand on his colder shoulder.

"Yes, but…" He shook his head. The long strands of his dark hair fell past his shoulders. "There is much, so much more that…" He shook his head almost in defeat. With a tired sigh he moved to a nearby chair and sat weakly within it.

"*Poupette*, there is danger for you, real danger. I have asked you to remain in this room for your safety – your protection. Please, I beg of you, do not venture out alone. I promise, in due course, all will be revealed. Everything will be made known to you. Until then, please, promise me that you will stay here until the time is right," Amadieu's voice beseeched her as his dark eyes held hers captive.

Nina felt the despair of her friend and could only capitulate. With an embarrassed nod of her head she moved to sit beside him. As the remorse poured from her, Amadieu wrapped an arm around her shoulder and hugged her.

"There, there now, *Poupette*," Amadieu cooed softly as he pulled her weeping form close. "It is so hard for a little bird to remain caged, I know. But in due course, you will see and know why I protect you so." His words brought comfort to her spirit.

For many days Nina honored her guardian's wishes. With each passing day she witnessed spring coming into full bloom from the window of her room. She spent her time reading the books Amadieu brought her, and she dreamt of the life continuing outside of the château. After what felt like an endless time,

Amadieu came to her room one night with important news. He would have to take leave of her for a short time, but he left plenty of food and water within her room. When he returned he hoped to have good news for her regarding something very dear to her. She questioned him and prodded, but he would not budge. Instead, he made her promise to remain in the safety of her room until his return. This is where she stayed, anxiously awaiting his return.

At first nothing unusual happened. There was simply the silence around her. Then, on the fourth night she heard a queer sound, something like a soft moan that reverberated through the stone walls. Nina found herself questioning her own hearing as she lifted her eyes from "The Tale of the Three Apples." When no further sound came, she shrugged her shoulders and continued to read about Caliph Harun al-Rashid. No sooner had her eyes returned to scanning the page than the noise was heard again.

The low lamentation came like the muffled wind against the château walls. She set the book aside, took a candle in hand and rose from her place. Moving to the door she put her hand upon it and leaned forward, placing her ear against the cold wood. When nothing was heard she slowly opened the door to the dark corridor. Drawn to the darkness, she took a tentative step into the hallway. She cocked her head and strained to listen for any sounds. Only the normal night noise rose from the darkness. From somewhere nearby she heard the gentle hum of the wind, and then it came again. It was so low, yet filled with such sorrow it tore at the young girl's heart.

Nina never thought of herself as an adventurous person, but on this night she found herself drawn to the soulful cries. With each step she took, the weeping grew louder. As she stood at the balcony of the stairs, she heard the sound echoing through the darkness of the château. With candle in hand, she searched upward to the third floor of the staircase.

By day Nina never thought of exploring the third floor of the château. Her youthful spirit only longed to bathe in the open sunlight. But tonight, as it neared the witching hour, she found herself mounting the spiral stairs. At the top she followed the mournful cry. Only when she came to the end of the hall did she feel the hair on the back of her neck rise. She lifted the candle high in hopes of seeing past the shadows, but they pressed in close swallowing up the weak light. When her eyes finally fell on a simple door, she moved to it. Once opened, Nina saw another hallway containing a narrow staircase leading upward into the attic.

Like a moth to a flame, she took a single step upon the rickety steps. Immediately the weeping grew silent. At the sudden change Nina grew deathly still. The interminable silence surrounded her with fear. With shaking hands she lifted her candle high in the vain hope of breaking through the pressing darkness.

Nina had never thought she would experience fear again. She never believed in the supernatural, nor did she think she held onto any superstitions, but on this day her entire psyche altered. Standing on the threshold of the staircase she peered up into the eyes of a demon. Like her nightmare from when she was ill, the creature stared down at her with blood red eyes and fanged teeth. She could not help but be reminded of the monsters that she saw on the banks of L'Isère River.

With a scream and a prayer, Nina dropped the candle where she stood and turned on the staircase. She had no conscious thought during the next interminable moments. Instinct alone, the instinct of prey running for its survival, moved her feet toward her room faster than they had ever before moved. The sound of bats fluttered behind her as she blindly made her way through the dark hallway to the corridor and straight to the light coming from her open room. Once inside her sanctuary, Nina slammed the large door shut on the phantom that chased her. In her panicked imagination she envisioned the soulless creature hovering outside her door. She could imagine it clawing at the wood in an attempt to gain entry, and then all fell silent except the harshness of her breath.

Nina felt the perspiration on her forehead. In a conscious move she bolted her door, then ran and jumped into her bed. Like a frightened schoolgirl, she pulled the covers over herself and burrowed into the bed. After a moment, she rose from the protection of the blankets and quickly drew the curtains around her bed closed. As if a second barrier, she made certain that no spectre from outside could see in before returning to the cocoon of blankets.

Sleep remained elusive that night and for many nights following. She began to understand Amadieu's warnings. Nina did not know what lay in the château's attic, but she did not ever want to witness it again. When sleep finally claimed her, she realized her dreams were taking her on a different journey.

The once peaceful dreams of an innocent girl were now replaced with images of a blood red death. She saw a life, not her own, pass before her eyes and on numerous occasions, her own screams of horror woke her up. Despite the nightmares she remained safely secure within her room. Too afraid to flee and abandon the château she spent the days in her room, and her nights fearful of the dreams that prevailed upon her psyche.

One night the moans and weeping lamentations echoed from the very walls of her room. Like she had on previous nights, Nina sat alone in the darkness with only the flames of the fireplace lighting the room. With the covers pulled around her head, she listened to the mournful sounds. By the single lamp she watched as the shadows swayed in hypnotic movements. Like the dance of veils, the gentle arches lulled her into their comforting embrace. Slowly, so slowly she did not notice it, her eyelids closed as her head bobbed downward. Before the blood red dreams of a succubus could take hold, she gasped in fear as she awakened with a chill.

Cautious of her surroundings, Nina glanced suspiciously into the shadows. Although the telltale sign of sweat was dripping down her brow she grasped the blanket closer like a valiant knight clinging to his shield. Her eyes darted off to the shadows searching for the unnatural phantom that waited patiently for her vigil to end.

Nina inhaled deeply as the pounding of her heart echoed off the walls. The rapid beating grew ever slower with each breath she took until finally, with weakened resolve, she felt the arms of Morpheus tugging her toward oblivion.

In the miasma of her dreams, Nina saw the all too familiar images surround her like a jilted lover. Painful touches morphed into pleasure. As the blackness turned red, the cold, foreboding fingers pulled her deeper under their spell. Like a raptor's talons, the sharp nails scraped over her delicate flesh, causing a gasp to escape her control.

Despite the exquisite sensations, Nina attempted resistance. Afraid of the rapturous pain sure to follow, she fought in vain against the unholy touch upon her. A still, small voice whispered tormenting words of longing and lust. With wanton abandon, she relinquished her chastity to become an unwilling mistress. When all seemed lost, she surrendered to the powers of darkness. Only then did she feel the painful pleasure that caused her nightly vigils. Although filled with fear, her body was unable to break free. With a climactic groan, she succumbed once again, to the sensuous grasp of the fiend within the shadows.

4 March, evening – Diary of Mademoiselle Cecilia Natashia Dupuin

It is so difficult to view my employer as a vibrant young woman, yet with the passing of her life story I can see how this château formed her into the person she has become. The trials through fear, the recollections of a woman close to the end of her life must truly have impacted her. I cannot help but wonder if all that she tells me is the truth or a wishful fantasy conjured by years of reading such tales. How did a young woman survive such an ordeal if it were true? Yet I cannot help believing. Madame Faivre is a kind and generous woman. Her words so far have rung true and the recent recollections of the fantastical events must also hold some truth, for what purpose would it be for such a grand dame to give herself up to such folly?

No, I must not judge. I am hired by Madame Faivre to transcribe the recollections of her life, and this I shall do, without judgment or prejudice. It is only fair.

5 March – The recollections of Madame Agnes (Nina) Brigitte Faivre

"You must think me mad to remain in such a diabolic place, yes? I assure you; I thought the same thing many times. As each day passed and Amadieu did not return, I wondered what I would do. The food he left, the bread, cured ham, cheese and water was beginning to dwindle, yet I remained." Madame Faivre's gaze grew reflective.

"But you must remember, child, I knew not where I was to go. The château was surrounded by the forest, and I was near Grenoble. However I did not know in which direction the hamlet lay. True, I could have tried to find my way back to Annecy, my village, but there was that forest with which to contend. How would I, so young and without knowledge of the land, fare in the dark forest?" Madame Faivre asked, expecting no answer.

"I did the only thing I could. I watched and waited. Every night those wailing lamentations pierced the château. My dreams were plagued with fantastic nightmares too ghastly to repeat." Her face screwed into something close to a grimace.

"Beg pardon, Madame, but some did not seem so ghastly," I reminded her as heat spread over my cheeks and colored them with a vibrant blush.

"Oh yes, you are right. Some were not so ghastly. Some, well, I shall keep them private." A bright hue colored Madame Faivre's cheeks. "In due course when you reach the brink of womanhood, I am sure you will understand such dreams yourself. Until then, let us continue our work. Let me tell you of my exploits from whence I left off, yes? Good, then let us continue the journey as best as I can recollect it," the elder matriarch said as she settled in to recount her days from long ago…

*****

The rations dwindled with each passing day and still Amadieu did not return. As the morning sun filtered into the room, Nina glanced out with longing at the nearby forest. Every night she listened to the frightful lamentation of an unknown fiend and was paralyzed with fear. But something changed that morning. Nina did not know what it was, but felt as if a silent resolve had settled in.

Nina knew she could not venture out into the forest. She did not known how far the town of Grenoble lay, and she was uncertain if she had enough supplies to last her on such a journey. Besides those issues, other concerns plagued her thoughts.

There was the beast in the attic to consider. With each passing night it continued to weep, Nina's memory of the accident slowly returned. She remembered the tale of *Celle qui pleure*, the spirit that lived near L'Îsère River and did not want to have another encounter with such a spectre. On top of this, the demons of that night might very well answer to such a ghostly woman, and Nina did not want to be anywhere near them, even by accident.

Nina kept this in mind as she paced the length of her room.

When her mind was made up, she took a candle and matches in hand and made her way from her room. The silence of the château might have been deafening if she had stopped to listen, but she did not. Filled with purpose she marched down the long corridor then up the spiraling staircase to the third floor.

"Papa always said that we much face our fears head on," Nina whispered as a way of fortifying her resolve.

The slight clipping of her shoes echoed through the third floor corridor. When she arrived at the end of the hall, she glanced at the single wooden door now closed. From somewhere a loud thumping resonated in her ears, and she realized it was the beating of her heart. Ignoring her own fears, she lit the candle and inhaled deeply. "I'm not afraid, Papa," she whispered as she touched the handle of the door.

With a gentle tug Nina felt the door open before her. Whatever phantom that once was there had now gone. All that remained was the silence of the stairwell. Like before, she held the candle high as she took the first tentative step upward. A litany of courageous phrases flowed through her mind as she made her way up the rickety stairs.

When Nina reached the top she was surprised to see the great length of an attic. The nearby windows were covered with tattered, fraying curtains, and in their condition it allowed the diffused light from outside to bathe the area. Nina moved into the attic and gazed at all of the wonders lying before her. Furniture of exquisite design sat nestled next to hand-carved wooden drawers, chassis, and bins.

Without thought Nina moved to a nearby window and pulled open the curtain. As the sun filled more of the attic, she continued to explore the area while pulling open the draped of every window. Caution was no longer her concern, and she moved freely through the room. Underneath a large tarp she found an immaculate mirror of such superb design that she could not help but gaze at her own reflection.

At seventeen Nina held a level of pride that allowed her to gaze at her own reflection. She noticed her youthful cheeks, once round and full with childhood plumpness were not growing thin and angular. Her cheekbones held a shape reminiscent of her mama, and her chin, almost too delicate to fathom, rested amiably. The dress she wore, a gift from Amadieu, clung to her budding form. Although not fancy, its material was of such design as to flatter the wearer. As she looked at her curves and bosom, Nina realized for the first time why her father used to look upon her with wistful sadness.

Nina was no longer a girl. Before the death of her mother and father she held an innocent quality. Not even being thrust into the status of an orphan caused her to age, but now, after her accident, many month of recovery and the time spent in the château she realized she had matured into a woman. Perhaps this was the wistful melancholy that settled upon her father, knowing one day his child, his beloved daughter, would be a woman and would begin to venture out into a life of her own.

At this thought Nina was humbled. Then a sudden sound caught her attention. Turning amongst the clutter of past memories she heard the scattering of small claws, then the familiar squeaking of the rats as they made way for her to pass. Cautious of where she stepped, she moved further into the attic. When she reached the end she gazed down upon a large oil canvas. On it was the portrait of a beautiful woman dressed in an emerald colored dress. The style was of a day long gone, and jewelry she wore held such vibrancy as to take one's breath away.

Nina could not help but gaze into the dark eyes of such a grand lady. She marveled at the way the mysterious woman smiled, the way that her cheeks creased upward into a warm and welcoming greeting. She had not ventured too far away from her home to be able to distinguish the different appearances of people, but she knew by looking at this woman that she was truly exotic. Nina wondered if she was perhaps Arab or Mediterranean, like the characters in many of her books.

Before she could dwell too long upon the picture, a squeaking came from nearby. As if directing her journey, the rat sat on its haunches. Its dark beady eyes seemed to glow as it scratched absently upon a large wooden chest. Ignoring its presence, Nina moved to the crate. Afraid of her, the creature scurried away with a fit of protesting squeaks.

Slowly opening the lid, Nina glanced back at the portrait of the woman and felt as if the woman's eyes encourage her exploits. She wondered who this woman was and what mysteries of the château would be uncovered. When she looked down into the chest, she found it filled with neatly bound bundles of correspondence. The papers were covered in dust and had faded with age. At first the girl did not know what to do, but as time elapsed and her courage grew, she took out the first bundle and read each one in turn. Only when she noticed the sun disappearing in the attic did she grab as many bundles of letters as she could carry. She closed the lid of the trunk and returned to her room.

It anyone had asked Nina, she would not have been able to explain her actions. All she knew was something compelled her movements. Like searching out the frightening lamentations which continued night after night, she could not help moving forward in her quest for knowledge. Although she had no proof, she believed these letters held answers to her questions. At least that was her fervent desire.

6 March, morning – Diary of Mademoiselle Cecilia Natashia Dupuin

So many questions arise with each passing day. I can seldom keep my patience in check. Each night when I go to sleep, I long for the end of dreams so I can begin a new day where Madame Faivre will reveal more of her wonderful life and the history of this château. In the evenings as I wander throughout the place I find myself wondering what mysteries lay in store for me. Perhaps like my employer I shall come across a secret room, an area that holds the key to all the answers yet to be discovered.

When I ventured to the same staircase Madame Faivre used to explore the attic, I found it blocked. Ever diligent, Frederic informed me that the third floor was off limits owing to the construction it required. The Madame had hoped to hire some workers in the spring in order to restore this level of the home, just as she has done to the rest of the place. Until then everyone was forbidden, owing to safety, from venturing onto the third floor. As I have no reason to doubt him, I simply move about the château at my leisure.

How queer it is to be walking the very steps my employer once walked. It is very strange to imagine the place void of life, yet her words confirm this. I wonder how it all changed. What caused the restoration of such a grand place, but more importantly, what could have brought about its previous ruin? So many questions left unanswered, and when I pose them to Madame Faivre she casts me a gentle smile and begs my patience.

"All in good time, all in good time."

It must be maddening for her to have such endless patience while I am nipping at her heels begging for more. Hopefully, in due course, it will be revealed to me.

Yet I find myself with mixed emotions on this topic. Once her tale is finished, my job will be over. This miraculous account of her past, the lingering images her words convey will be finished and my employment complete. There will be no need for me to remain in the presence of such a grand lady.

How cruel life can be to find me such a wonderful soul and then snatch it away. I am sorely tempted to slow my rate of transcribing but I know I cannot do this. It would not be honorable to prolong the task in order to simply stay within the company of such a kind soul as Madame Faivre. So I will do as I must. I will continue to transcribe her words, and when the tale is complete I shall sadly move on and allow this gentle old lady her privacy once again.

9 March – The recollections of Madame Agnes (Nina) Brigitte Faivre

"You might wonder why I begged some days of privacy, yes?" were the first words that greeted me. "Well, it is no secret my child, no secret at all. You see, I am an old lady and I tire easily. Besides, did it not give you time to explore as only a youth could?" Madame Faivre asked, then smiled when she saw the red hue form on my cheeks.

"I beg pardon, Madame," I began to apologize as I remembered my wanderings through her grand estate.

"Child, do not blush. I have heard of your wanderings through our château and am grateful that you enjoy it as much as we do. Yes, to find such a place splendid is indeed a gift that you give to my poor old heart. To know that you walk through the snow-covered garden softly to yourself is a treasure to my ears. Oh yes, I hear you through my open window. Yes, it is chilly, but I do so love the scent of the approaching spring." Her eyes drifted to the nearby window as a slight smile crossed her lips.

The sound of the gardeners could be heard through the window. Their low voices were respectful as they moved about their business.

I almost spoke casually, but when I looked at Madame Faivre, I noticed her eyelids slowly drooping. "If you are falling asleep, perhaps you would prefer to rest, Madame?" My voice pulled her from whatever trance her mind began to conjure.

"What? Oh, no child, no. I was not falling asleep, merely remembering the vibrant colors of spring. Why, if I close my eyes I can see the radiant hues of orange, yellow, and white that litter my garden with such a canopy of fragrance. I hope, dear one, that you will see such beauties. I am very proud of my garden and the treasures that it holds." Her hand rested lightly on mine, and I could not help but inform her of the garden at Madame Ségolène's school.

"What is that? There was a garden at your school? Oh, how wonderful that you enjoyed your time in such a garden. I am not certain if mine can equal what you left behind, but hopefully you will find merit in it." Madame Faivre smiled warmly.

"Madame, I am certain that nothing could equal the beauty of your garden," I assured her.

"Yes, you are sweet to compliment it so, but you have not seen it at the full height of spring. Soon, I can feel it in my bones; very soon you shall be witness to the new life that spring brings forth. How I hope you enjoy it as much as I do. But enough talk about my garden. You wish to know more of my life, yes? Then come, my dear child, prepare yourself, and I shall pick up where we left off. Though I warn you, the rest becomes a bit...risqué. Oh, let me tell you. Those letters I came across were quite educational for one as innocent as I." Madame Faivre's voice grew low as if conveying a scandal. All I could do was avert my eyes to my steno pad and I prepared to transcribe. Noticing my discomfort, Madame Faivre patted my hand reassuringly.

"But I cause you to blush. Enough of this talk. Let me begin to explain of my great find, for a truly great discovery it was." She spoke softly like a conspirator as her words took me back to that time from long ago...

*****

The first thing Nina did once returning to the sanctuary of her room was to place the bundled letters in chronological order. Those that she had read were placed near the end, being the most current writings. When she determined which letters were the first, she gently removed the cloth ribbon holding the bundle together and began to read. Just as she became lost in the many stories from the novels, she found herself swept away in the words written many years ago.

Nina had never read such elegant lines before. She did not know that such depth of love and devotion could exist between two people, let alone between two women. But as she opened each letter, the words flowed freely and carried her away.

The first letter began innocently enough from a Comtesse Laurensa Catherine de la Fontaine. The words, almost too polite for the paper, flowed freely in neat script.

23 January 1798

Isabelle, Baronne de la Chorange,
It is with gratitude that I thank you for your hospitality. As I am a recent widow, it has healed my heart greatly to know that your kindness was near. The understanding you displayed for my need of solitude by day, and quiet reflections at night have allowed me to see that not all is lost after the death of my husband, the Comte. If the kindness could ever be repaid, you have only to beckon.

Your Friend,
Comtesse Laurensa Catherine de la Fontaine

At last the mystery of who laid buried in the cemetery was being revealed, yet with every answered question Nina discovered more mysteries. By the letters' account, Isabelle, Baronne de la Chorange, did not live at the château near Grenoble but resided at her own home near the city of Avignon. Exactly how the two met was unclear to Nina, but the letters gave a full recounting of the friendship that developed between the two.

With each new letter a broader understanding emerged.

Nina found herself delving deeper and deeper into the story of love and devotion. The fact that the words were written between women meant little to her as she moved quickly through the letters.

27 March 1798

My dearest Laurensa,

It is with great sadness and gratitude that I tell you how lucky you are. I know it is difficult to see beyond the loss of your beloved husband, taken in the prime of his manhood. Yet as I ponder the days since last I read your words, I find myself filled with such longing that my situation was different. No, may the good Lord forgive my thoughts, I wish no ill upon my husband. But life in his château is so very different from my own home in Bordeaux. Without kin or kith I find myself truly alone, save in these words that we share.

I always knew that, as the eldest daughter, much would be expected of me, yet I did not realize how much until now. So many days have gone by since I lay with my husband in our marriage bed that remains fruitless. How fortunate that your husband never placed such expectations upon you, my dearest friend. Already I heard the smirks of the servants who comment on the lack of our blessings.

Know, my beloved friend, that if only I could, I would give my husband what he wishes, but God has not seen fit to bless me as He did the Blessed Virgin. I shall go to the prêtre again and ask for penitence in hopes that God may forgive me my transgressions. Soon, my dearest Laurensa, I hope to convey upon you the honorary title of Aunt, for how much you have become dear to my heart.

Yours faithfully,
Isabelle, Baronne de la Chorange

Nina felt the sorrow as if it were her own. Almost seventeen, she knew the importance of children. More importantly she understood what it meant for a woman of rank to issue forth children. There was a part of her that felt for the Baronne, the woman buried long ago. Without skipping a beat, she took the next letter and began to read the reply to the Baronne's heart-felt words.

14 April 1798

My dearest Isabelle,
I have read your letter several times, and I am fraught with anger at the thought that any-one, least of all a servant, be so cruel to you. How beastly it is that a man should wage his guilt upon his wife for their lack of fruit. Nay, my dear Isa-belle, you did not have to proclaim this for I know that a servant's tongue only wags the words of his master. How abominable of him to allow others, let alone servants, to believe that your lack of issue is your sin to bear. Isabelle, this is not your sin, it is not your curse! Do not allow that man who is your husband to beat you so, for indeed words can be as harsh as a fist.

Pray tell, my beloved, he is not a violent man? Were he to be, I would rush with all due haste and pluck you from his place. You do not deserve such a beast. Were you with me, I would never let a day go by without allowing you to feel how worthy you truly are. My dearest, my beloved, you are a friend most dear to me yet you are so much more. All you need do is beckon, and I shall be there by your side. My château is modest compared to your abode in Avignon, but there is ample room for two mistresses. We can live in the peaceful harmony as only two bosom friends could.

Always yours,
Comtesse Laurensa Catherine de la Fontaine

Nina found herself blushing after reading this letter. She felt both the pain and anger of the Comtesse, yet another emotion began to surface, amazed bewilderment. Yes, she knew of bosom friends, she herself had had many while growing up, but these words, the proclamations were taking a decidedly different turn.

As if not realizing how much time had gone by, she glanced at her open window and noticed the darkness. She did not know if the witching hour was upon her, nor did she care. Instead Nina rose from her place by the fire and closed the shutters to her window. When the curtains were drawn she felt the room become warm. When a stifled yawn escaped her control, she moved back to the scattered letters. She contemplated reading further but as the fatigue grew, she decided to set them aside for now. Tomorrow would be a new day and by daylight it would be easier to continue her exploration into the lives of these two women.

It had been over a week, and Amadieu had not yet returned. She wondered if he would become angry with her for reading these correspondences, but then decided that he might not care. They were, after all, yet more reading to occupy her time. With this thought she made herself ready for bed.

While she secretly hoped to dream of the lives of these two women, Nina found her dreams taking an entirely different turn. From somewhere in her subconscious mind she heard the familiar sound of a soul in pain. The tears and weeping filled the entire château and seeped into the recesses of her mind. Over and over again, she felt the pain of the Baronne and wondered if it was her ghost that remained held, a prisoner for all time, in the confines of the attic.

10 March, morning – Diary of Mademoiselle Cecilia Natashia Dupuin

There is happiness in Madame Faivre that is unexpected. As she was speaking of the letters between the two women I caught her, several times, glancing my way. Once or twice she stopped completely as if gauging my reaction, but I gave none. Instead I kept my concentration focused as I transcribed all of her words.

I wonder what emotion she expected from me. Did she think that I would be repulsed by the idea of love between two women? Or did she think me so naïve that I would not understand the full ramifications of her words? How odd it is that she would think that I, an educated woman of Paris, would cast judgment upon this tale.

The love of two women is not unknown to me. The innocent flirtations that I and my bosom friend, Margarie, shared were common in the girl's academy. Those long, lonely nights in our room in which we shared in mutual explorations of each other could not be forgotten. Sometimes rumors surfaced regarding one particular schoolmarm and another, and although none had proof, I know that there must have been a few who held special affections for each other. But I could not say this to Madame Faivre. She is, after all, my first employer. What if such news came as queer to her? No, it is better that I remain silent and diligent. In time, perhaps when the tale is finished, I will be able to explain to her that those in my generation are far more lenient than they were in hers.

Until then, all I can do is the very best job that I am able.

10 March – The recollections of Madame Agnes (Nina) Brigitte Faivre

"You must think me strange for reading those most private letters, but I have to tell you, once I began to read them my loneliness was dispelled. I found myself pulled into this great romance that not even I had ever heard of before. Even to this day I cannot help but go back to those letters to read their powerful words of heartfelt devotion." Madame Faivre's voice became solemn, then she glanced at me, a slight smile curving her lips.

"Oh yes, you look at me strangely, but I assure you, it was a tale of love and romance. The emotion, the feelings, they exist. What should it matter that is was two women who loved? Does this make their emotions any less real? Well, let me tell you, it did not to me. I found myself intrigued beyond imagination," Madame Faivre defended her actions from years ago.

"Madame, I do not mean to offend. I do understand. It's just that I have never heard of it spoken openly," I tried to explain myself.

Madame Faivre glanced at me as if attempting to read my sincerity. With a nod of her head, she sighed. "You have to understand, child, that in those days things were different. Oh, I read of love between a man and a woman. I knew the mechanics of it, as you will. I had even heard the whispers of love rumored to be between two women. A few times I might have even had such a bosom love for a friend when I was a child. But reading their love letters gave me insight that I never before imagined. It was amazing to see their devotion grow stronger with each passing day." Her voice held a wistful note when she continued her explanation.

"There was a part of myself that wished to feel such love. I longed to have someone profess such words for me. If only I could have someone wanting to rescue me, why, I would have been the happiest girl ever." Madame Faivre crackled with laughter.

"So this is how it was. The love between Laurensa and Isabelle is one that warmed my heart during those early spring days. For them, their love blossomed in their letters over the spring and by autumn, things were beginning to change. I knew that if I just kept reading, perhaps the answers would be revealed," she explained as she got a wistful expression.

"Now, looking back I realize how naïve I truly was. The constant noise in the attic every night, the lamentations and weeping I thought to be the ghost of either Laurensa of Isabelle. I realized how said their lots in life must have been and this made me feel their pain greatly. Yes, very truly sad, child. As naïve as I was, I believed if only I could understand the pain, then perhaps I could release the spirit to the arms of our Maker." Her voice became soft and distant remembering that time.

"But this is a different story, perhaps for another time. For now let me go further into my life, for the story begins to take shape and soon all will be explained," she said as her words began to weave the story of days from long ago…

*****

Throughout the letters from the spring Nina found herself in a perpetual blush. Her cheeks warmed at the explicit words of love between the two women. Their fondness for each other, the constant terms of endearment grew stronger with each passing refrain.

5 June 1798

My darling Laurensa,
I write with heavy heart, for I have spoken to the father at my chapel. I have told him of my love for you, and he has stated that it is unnatural, and abomination against God. Yet how can such pure emotions be an abomination? How can what I feel in my heart, this unending love and desire for you, my dearest friend, offend God?
As I am unable and unwilling to free you from my affections, I find myself at the church giving daily penitence for this love we share. Perhaps in time, my dear sweet Laurensa, my mind will be clear to know which path I shall journey. My heart beckons me to you, yet my nature, this damnable resource that is a part of my birth, chains me to a loveless marriage and a man who judges my worth upon the children that have yet to be born.
Think of me, my dear friend, during this time of turbulent confusion.

You dearest friend,
Isabelle, Baronne de la Chorange

21 June 1798

My most beloved friend, Isabelle,

I lament at your struggles and wish that I could wipe them away. I invite you, freely, to come to my abode. The situation you find yourself in is deplorable at best. Yet I feel, my sweet friend, that there is much that I have yet to tell you.

The first and foremost is that I do not hold sway to the prattles of the Church or the teachings of your God. Perhaps as a child I was once like you, but now I am an adult and have put away such childish ways. This philosophy is one that I shared with my late husband. Neither one of us felt the blessings of God, and even today, with all that has transpired, I know that God is no friend of mine.

Pray that I do not offend you, my dearest friend. I have many reasons for these convictions, all of which you should understand. I am an abomination, a hellish fiend if ever there was, and if it were in your priest's hand to dictate, I would be wiped away like a scourge on the earth. No, my sweet Isabelle, you have not met the full wrath of your beliefs as have I. I tell you now truly, earnestly, and sincerely, were you to come to me now you, too, would be persecuted by the hand of your God.

Think well on this, my beloved. I long to aid you in your times of trouble, but you must know the truth. You must be fully aware of all decisions made and accord them as your heart desires.

Until then, I am forever your humble friend, Comtesse Laurensa Catherine de la Fontaine

30 June 1798

My dear, sweet Laurensa,
What has caused such wrath from you toward my benevolent God? As sure as I am that my penitence shall be received, I am certain that you, for whatever sins you might harbor, are as dear to God as a pure, innocent child. You are so good, my dear friend. You have reached out your hand when no other would. You call out to me, and I hear your voice. Even in my deepest despair it is as if your touch is upon me. Please, do not grow too harsh, for I know that God will surely see favor on us. I know not how or when, but I must hold on to faith, for it is all I have.

You beloved friend,
Isabelle, Baronne de la Chorange

13 July 1798

My sweet and innocent Isabelle,
If only you knew the darkness that exists. If only you understood the true evil that surrounds us daily, you would not hold out hope, for I have lost it. Once I was like you, filled with idealistic dreams of a benevolent creator. I used to laugh freely and live life with vigor every day. But you see, my beloved, I was deceived.

The curse that we share, my lovely Isabelle, is that we were born of Eve. As such, our lots are cast long before we grow weary of our mother's milk. Yes, like you, I was given over to a man of noble bearing, and, like you, I was deceived and betrayed by my own kin.

I wish I could explain the truest darkness of Hell, but it is indescribable. Let it simply be said that my husband was the greatest deceiver, and I, upon his demise, did not shed a tear.

How I wish I could turn back the hands of time and end it all before it began, but alas, it is too late. Now I am forever damned, and there is naught to do but wait and hope for a better tomorrow, if indeed there is one.

Pray tell you ask no more; simply know that I would never upon my wretched soul cast the shadow over you that has been placed upon me. You are far too beloved of me to ponder this. The purity of your spirit is what I adore and cherish most.

Your most beloved friend,
Comtesse Laurensa Catherine de la Fontaine

23 July 1798

Sweet, cherished Laurensa,
Pray tell what has darkened your heart so? You who are so pure and loving, to have such emotions toward yourself. It seems like only a short while ago that you were here with me, laughing and partaking of my hospitality. Even your presence cheered the downward mood of my husband. Surely you must know what a pure blessing you are. No, my beloved, you are not damned. You are my ever sweet and loving Laurensa. There is no shadow that you could possibly cast upon me that I would not welcome. And I, your benevolent friend, would dearly love to shower the goodness and sunshine upon you, if it were only within my power.

But, my dear, dear friend, I must give you good news.

Just days ago I was in the chapel alone. My heart was bleeding for your pain and sorrow, and all I could ponder was our lamentable condition. This love we share, this longing within us can only be met with penitence, or so I thought.

Laurensa, dear sweet Laurensa, do not yet grieve. Please, prey read my words for the earnest nature they are intended.

As I was weeping softly holding my rosary and whispering the Hail Mary a kind gentle friar came to kneel beside me. He knew not who I was nor cared my station in life, he simply felt my sorrow and longed to alleviate some of the mantle of suffering. So kind and gentle was he that I beseeched him to stay in my humble home, which you know has many empty rooms. After much cajoling, he indeed returned with me, and from him I learned a great deal.

Laurensa, he is a monk, a poor man who re-nounced wordly goods in search of peace and en-lightenment. He comes from a small abbey near the town of Genoa. He passed through our town on a pilgrimage to Santiago de Compostela in Spain

Laurensa, how blessed am I that this poor man crossed my path? Over the days I spoke candidly to him. I explained my lamentations in full confi-dence. In return he told me stories from the Holy Scriptures. I learned of a warrior and his songs for a beloved soldier, and Laurensa, there is a love shared between two of the most heartfelt women that I have ever heard of. One gave the following declaration to the other, 'Intreat me not to leave thee, or to return from following after thee: for whither thou goest, I will go; and where thou lodg-est, I will lodge: thy people shall be my people.'

Please, do not despair my truest friend. All will be well.

> *Your ever loving friend,*
> *Isabelle, Baronne de la Chorange*

3 August 1798

My sweet, sweet Isabelle,

Can this be true? Is there hope? Could there be redemption for us yet? Pray, do say the words that I long to hear. Through all of my dark nights I only long for you. I fervently desire you, my beloved. I am alone in this world. If I were to be granted one blessing, it would be your warm hand in mine.

The very walls of my château seem to whisper your name. The lonely empty corridors long for your presence. I beg of you, my dearest friend, do not drift away. Do not allow the world to take you from me. Please, my beloved, let me hear your voice. Come, my love, and hold me in your arms. I pledge myself to you forever, my sweet, Isabelle. You are all that I am searching for. Do not let this evil take you far away from me.

I beseech you, my dear sweet Isabelle, call for me. Reach for me now. My most beloved, you are my heart's desire. For so long my blood ran cold with despair, but now you have given it renewed life. Do not allow the storm of our circumstances to tear us asunder. All that I want is your warmest presence. Do not turn away from me, my dear sweet Isabelle. Come and let me hold you close within my embrace.

I beg of you, say the words and I shall spirit you away.

Anxiously waiting, You Beloved,
Comtesse Laurensa Catherine de la Fontaine

17 August 1798

My beloved Laurensa,
For whither thou goest, I will go; and where thou lodgest, I will lodge: thy people shall be my people.

> *Counting the days, your truest,*
> *Isabelle, Baronne de la Chorange*

The piles of letters ended here. Surprised, Nina move through her room in search for bundles she might have missed. Almost frantic, she tossed sheets of paper aside in hope of learning more. But on this night, there would be no more revelations. Instead she fell asleep exhausted and dreaming of the love shared between two women.

11 March, morning – Diary of Mademoiselle Cecilia Natashia Dupuin

How grand it must be to have a love such as that. As I sat up late transcribing Madame Faivre's words, I wondered at this affair that took place so many years ago. How did it end? Were they able to live happily ever after as I have read in so many children's tales?

But those books were different. Those stories held vastly different scenarios and the love interest was always between a man and a woman. What must have happened to the two noble women from so long ago?

Lately I find myself wondering if Margarie and I could have survived such trials, but then I tell myself no. Our love was the love shared of youthful innocence when we had no others to whom to turn. Two orphans alone in the world could only cleave to each other. As we grew older and our proclivities transformed, it was only natural our childhood dreams would no longer include each other. I understand this now, but still, I wonder, is there someone for me? Like Isabelle longed for her Comtesse, I long for someone to love and hold. If these two could find each other in this vast and ever changing land, then who could be out there for me, I wonder?

This morning as I dressed, Amadieu entered my quarters. There was no knock, nor prior warning, he simply opened the door, entered my room, gave a pleasant greeting, and removed the tea kettle from last night. I do not mind his intrusions and honestly do not see them as such. Since my arrival Amadieu has been the kindest to me, next to Frederic.

Amadieu with his piercing dark eyes. Amadieu with his jet black hair and handsome features.

For a while I began to wonder, but then quickly dispensed with the notion. Amadieu is a friend, as dear a friend as one could be. His inclinations do not lay with the fair sex. He never said this to me, but I can tell. Even with the little schooling I had, I noticed his looks at Frederic and the other male servants. I saw the gazes he cast upon the men who worked outdoors. Amadieu preferred the company of men.

As if hearing my thoughts Amadieu turned towards me. His gaze held me hostage as a wry smile crossed his lips. Not for the first time I noticed the sharp canine teeth that sat longer than the bridge of his upper teeth. With the curtains still drawn against the early spring chill, all lanterns were lit, and it seemed as if it caused a slight glow to his form.

"Will there be anything else," he asked me, which caused me to blush at my previous musing. I gulped down my fear as I returned my gaze to the transcripts on my desk.

"Ummm, no, thank you, Amadieu," was all I could mumble before he left.

I am not all together certain but I could have sworn that I heard a soft chuckle from him. It was as if he laughed at my very embarrassing thoughts. But as I contemplated this I knew that I must be hearing things. My thoughts are my own, and I know it is silly to think that my friend could hear them. No, I am certain that he was not laughing at my expense.

11 March – The recollections of Madame Agnes (Nina) Brigitte Faivre

"You are probably wondering what happened to the two? I know I did. For many days I reread the letters. I thought over the situation and contemplated all that I knew. The Baronne was buried in the family plot of Laurensa Catherine de la Fontaine. But what of the Comtesse? What would have befallen her, I wondered." Madame Faivre echoed my thoughts.

"Was she successful? Did she whisk her great love back to her château and then for one reason or another, leave and pass away too far from her home? Oh yes, child. Like you, I found my mind constantly churning with question and question. Ultimately there was not much to do. All of the letters had been read twice, sometimes three times. There were no clues for me and the silence held no answers either. So there I sat, night after night waiting for my friend to return. By day I ventured into the château, but never at night. Then one night after a particular nightmare I got my courage up. I decided that the answers lay with the lamenting spirit of the apparition in the attic. Yes, I had decided to face the ghostly spirit head on." Madame Faivre's words were filled with conviction as she began to recount that time from long ago...

*****

The soulful sounds of weeping poured through the corridors. Like before, Nina moved cautiously toward the noise. With candle in hand she carefully opened the door leading to the attic. Fearful of seeing the fiendish creature again, she took a hesitant step forward. When nothing happened, she moved a bit faster but with great caution.

The spirits and phantoms of the night were always dispersed by day and Nina was never afraid to wander through this cluttered place. But now, in the heart of darkness, she walked softly in an attempt to make as little noise as possible. When she heard the aching cries again, she stopped to get her bearing. With a slight tilt of her head, she listened for the muted echo and when she heard it, she moved closer to the canvas portrait leaning against the farthest wall. As she approached she heard the sounds of sniffling, then the deep guttural moan of one in pain. Only when she got close enough did she stop, frozen in place.

Sitting upon the ground was a woman she had never seen before. With a candelabrum by her side, the stranger faced the portrait of the smiling woman. From where she stood Nina could not see this woman's features, but she noticed her long, dark hair fell nearly to her waist. If she did not know better, she would have wondered if this was Amadieu jesting with her. However, upon closer inspection, Nina noticed the woman's curves. True, wearing men's breeches and long white shirt, Nina would be hard pressed to recognize the form as a woman. But even dressed like this, with the candles sitting opposite her, Nina could see the gentle shadowed outline of bosoms below the white cotton shirt.

"Oh, my dear sweet one." The grieving words cut through the silence. "Too long, my love, too long without you. We had so little time together, and now I am truly alone." The woman wept.

Nina took a tentative step but froze when she heard the woman's next words.

"Oh my Isabelle, my very own love. How we were so happy, so content." The words were a mere whisper.

In that instant Nina felt a shiver cross her spine. Her vision tunneled, and all she could see was the back of this woman who could only be one person. As if smelling her fear, the stranger suddenly turned and rose to her full height. It was then that she came face to face with Comtesse Laurensa Catherine de la Fontaine.

"You!" The fiend of old returned as the woman's shape transformed before Nina's eyes. "Leave me be!" came her ordered scream.

"I-I..." but Nina found her voice gone, her ability to speak suddenly lost.

As the creature moved toward her, Nina prayed for a quick death, but it was not meant to be. Instead, she heard her own high-pitched scream as she dropped the candle and fled from the attic. Each heart-pounding footstep felt like an eternity. At one point she felt a sharp talon cut the back of her dress. With a terror-filled scream she made her way through the corridor and down the spiral staircase.

If she had been of her right mind, she would have run back

to the safety of her room just as she did before. Instead she was running for her life as her mind tried in vain to understand all that had happened.

The love affair took place so long ago. The image of the woman on the canvas was one of youth and beauty and the stranger, the creature lamenting before the canvas was as young as Amadieu. Her mind screamed for answers even as her body cried out for sanctuary from the hideous beast that chased her through the château.

Without direction, she ran as fast as she could. The dark night did little to hide her from the beast. At one point she realized she had broken through a door. The cold air bit against her flesh even as she screamed in terror. From somewhere behind her she felt the fiend nearing, but continued to run in a vain attempt at freedom. Only when she stood within the family cemetery did she stop to catch her breath. All around her was the silence of the night.

Panting and out of breath, Nina gazed at the headstones nearby. Disoriented she moved toward the circular landscape where the main crypt was located. Once inside the circle, she looked up at the marble statues of angels and saw them gazing down at her, accusing her of her trespasses. With a disbelieving shake of her head, she stumbled further into the hallowed ground. As she moved before the private mausoleum, she gazed up at the guardian angel that continually wept. By the reflection of the clear moonlight she saw, for the first time, the statue slowly moving. No longer hiding its weeping face, it sat up and gazed down at her with impenetrable eyes. As if weeping for her soon demise, streaks of blood red tears fell heedless down its marble cheeks.

Nina felt her mind turning inward. The hideousness of the situation was causing her mental faculties to shut down one by one. Before she could feel the total blackness consume her, two strong hands clasped her shoulders. She quickly turned and almost screamed, but Amadieu's features brought a cry of relief.

"Oh Amadieu!" she wept as she wrapped her arms around his neck. He held her close and cooed softly, but then gently pulled her from his form. When she looked up at him she saw his eyes moving toward a nearby plot.

"Amadieu?" Her voice was a bare whisper.

"Shush now, *Poupette*. All is well," Amadieu whispered as he began to pull her behind him protectively.

"Amadieu, what have I said of your little pet?" a woman's voice rose from the darkness. Her voice was a combination of a bark and reptilian hiss with anger etching every word.

Struck by fear, the tall man knelt as he bowed his head humbly. Confused, Nina looked up expecting to see the fiend that had chased her. Instead she saw the woman from the attic. Holding the candelabrum, the stranger towered above them, her black boots planted firmly in the snow. In that moment, Nina noticed the woman's apparel. She noticed how the men's breeches clung tightly to the stranger's curves. The shirt once loose was now neatly tucked within the waist. Like magic, the wind swirled around the Comtesse causing her long, dark tresses to fly in the breeze. When Nina looked up into the woman's face, she did not see her exquisite beauty. Instead she saw the glowing red eyes of a demon from Hell.

"My lady, forgive me. The child is young; I should never have left her unattended for so long," Amadieu offered as he tugged at Nina until she knelt beside him.

Her eye never left the tall woman's. Instead she felt her mind spiraling out of control. With little ado Nina swooned and, with a thud, fell face first into the wet, muddy grass.

12 March, morning – Diary of Mademoiselle Cecilia Natashia Dupuin

I can scarcely believe what I transcribed. How could this be? Is it true, or is it the effects of senility? I do not know, but I must stay true to my profession. I must record Madame Faivre's account, and silently I shall pray that my poor employer did not experience the horrors imagined.

What an utterly sad fate, if it be true.

But as I recollect I find it hard to believe that ill fate met with Madame Faivre. She now lives in the lap of luxury. Although not titled, she holds control of this wonderful château. There are servants who see to her every need. Yet what happened on that night so long ago? What could she have seen that caused such fright?

To my surprise Amadieu is scarce. He seems intent on avoiding my presence and perhaps he knows I would query him. Already I find myself filled with myriad questions left unanswered.

Madame Faivre has begged my patience once more. She wished to rest a short while before we resume. This waiting is enough to cause insanity, for I fear there is much more left to learn.

Thankfully with spring approaching I can venture outdoors for jaunts. Off in the distance I hear the waters of L'Îsère River and wonder how far a journey it is. The forest that once caused fear in a teen now only looms with lush, beautiful trees. Somewhere deep in the forest I hear the sound of the men's hunting party, their guns echoing through the air, and I know that tonight's dinner will consist of a plump pheasant or other fowl.

Yes, how queer it all is. How strange yet magical is this château. I find myself morbidly intrigued with its story, yet fearful of what I might learn. How strange to have such duality in a single place.

27 March, morning – Diary of Mademoiselle Cecilia Natashia Dupuin

Madame Faivre has requested I join her in her boudoir. She wishes to resume transcribing even though she does not feel well. I begged her to reconsider, but she would hear none of it. So I made her vow a promise that the moment she tired, we would stop the session.

She is a stubborn old woman, and I write this fondly. She is filled with such fire and conviction not even ill health will stop her. So I go, for the first time, to site by her bedside. Like her nurse I shall sit vigil, not to monitor her health, but to write down every word.

27 March – The recollections of Madame Agnes (Nina) Brigitte Faivre

"Come child, come and sit closer." Madame Faivre lay upon a soft bed with the elegantly rich coverlet drawn up. "The open window does not cause you a chill, does it?"

"No Madame, it is refreshing." I smiled softly.

"Good, good. I am glad. At my age I wish to look out at the coming sky of spring. It is so wonderful and so very different from all the other seasons. It is deep blue and clean. It reminds me of life, all of the newborns that will soon arrive. Did you hear the birds in the trees during your wandering?"

Madame Faivre spoke as if this were a normal transcription session, and I answered as softly as I could lest my voice alone cause her pain.

"Good, good. I am glad that you appreciate them as I do. The birds are so dear to me, but I have a special place in my heart for the sparrows. Their songs are filled with joy, even the night birds seem to sing a pleasant song." Madame Faivre smiled and then turned her attention to the nurse sitting in the room.

"Yes, this place, this château is dear to my heart as are all who reside in it." Her voice grew gentle as if conveying a message. When the nurse gave a fond smile, Madame Faivre returned her gaze to the open window. Sensing my presence once again, the elderly woman smiled at me.

"But I am rambling, yes?"

"No, not at all," I assured as I readied my pen to transcribe.

"Very well. You wish to hear the rest of the story. I know it has been very difficult for you, my child, waiting and wondering, not knowing what is to come next. I promise, you will have all the answers that you desire for this shall be the final transcription you will take."

I could not help but express my surprise and disappointment. "Madame, surely it does not end so soon? Madame, are you well? Please do not tell me that ill health will end our visits." My voice shook at the thought of my employment, and friendship, ending so soon.

"What?" she asked with confusion at my question, then smiled indulgently when I asked my question again.

"Oh, my dear girl, I have no plans to go anywhere. It is simply that the story ends. When it ends, there is nothing left to do but to begin another story anew," she explained with a smile before turning her concentration to the task at hand.

"Come now and listen to the ramblings of my life," she coaxed as she began her narration of her days from long ago...

*****

Nina paced hysterically to and fro. She did not listen to a word that Amadieu said. Instead she was raging as only a seventeen year old could rage. When she was spent, she fell backwards onto her bed.

"Are you quite finished now?" Amadieu's voice sounded bored.

"I am sure there is more but I grow weary," Nina allowed the sarcasm to sound. "When were you going to tell me, Amadieu?" she asked.

"Tell me what?" That you are alive today by the good graces of my mistress, the Comtesse?" his voice bit back.

She sat up in bed and looked across the room at him. Nina expected to see the anger in his features but instead she saw calmness settled in his firm jaw. He absently picked at his trousers, then looked up and met her gaze.

"The Comtesse, she is a... she is not... that is to say," Nina's words stumbled past her lips. She shook her head once more as she rose to slowly pace the room. In an unconscious manner she bit on the corner of her thumbnail.

"*Poupette*, please do not bite your nails. Do you know how long it took me to manicure them?" Amadieu's voice pleaded.

"Amadieu, what did she mean 'your pet'? Is that all I am to you?" Nina turned to her friend, her voice calm.

"What do you think?" He gazed at her, a soft smile creasing his lips.

"I thought you were my friend, my savior." Her brows furrowed into a frown.

"Well, I never considered myself much of a savior, but a friend. Yes, I am your friend and always will be." He smiled as he stood up and moved before her. "You are not my pet."

"Then why did she say that?"

Amadieu turned away and moved to the open window. The clear night sky sent a cool breeze into the room. As if searching for an answer, he stared into the darkness.

"The Comtesse is not well; she is ill. No, not like you imagine. She is sick of heart. She has been in deep mourning for sometime and nothing will free her from it." He turned to Nina and watched her closely. "*Poupette*, she did not mean what she said, and when she realizes her words, there will not be another person who judges herself more harshly than she."

Nina heard the sincerity in his words, yet found them hard to believe. "How can you say that, Amadieu? How can you be so, so compassionate toward such a fiend! She is evil, Amadieu. She is a monstrous creature that deserves nothing but scorn! I saw her, Amadieu; I saw the creature that she becomes! She nothing but a ruthless, evil fiend!" Nina moved closer to her friend.

"Amadieu, please, I am well now. The Comtesse does not move by day, let us, you and I, leave this place. We can go first thing in the morning." She beseeched him softly and wrapped her arms around his lean for. His back grew stiff at her touch, but he did not pull away. Then, with a slight frown he turned to her.

"Poupette, would you call me those things, too? Am I a monster who deserves only your scorn?" Sadness filled his dark eyes.

"What? No, of course not. Amadieu, you are my dear friend, never would I see you as a monster. You are not like her. You cannot help that you are her servant, but even she, in today's age, should know that servants are free to move on if they desire," Nina stated with conviction.

"Nina, *Poupette*, you do not understand." He took her warm hands within his cold ones. "I am her servant by choice. I am free to come and go, and yes, I am exactly like the Comtesse." His voice was tender.

"But..." Nina found herself suddenly remembering a dream from long ago. The nightmare by L'Îsère River after the accident when the mob of demons surrounded her, returned with full force. She had almost been taken away by the *Celle qui pleure* that night, but was rescued by a vision she could not remember. In the back of her mind she suddenly saw that night clearly. There was a shadowy figure, a creature that slithered through the mud like a carnivore – a fiend. And then she knew.

"Amadieu," she whispered as realization settled in.

She suddenly remembered the blood red eyes that looked down at her. When she gazed into Amadieu's eyes she felt a sudden familiarity. As he nodded in acknowledgement she remembered the dream she had shortly after arriving at the château. All this time she though that the hallucination of a monster on her ceiling was the result of a fever, now, with the truth known, she felt her heart beating loudly in her ears.

"Amadieu?" her voice betrayed her.

"Yes, *Poupette*. The Comtesse and I are the same. We are both vampires, creatures of the night, who are worthy only of your scorn. Is that not what you said?" His voice was filled with sadness.

"Oh Amadieu." She found herself shaking her head. Her heart was breaking for the sadness she caused her friend. When his words finally registered, she moved and sat on the settee. "How, Amadieu?"

"How did it happen? To her or me?" he smiled as he moved and flopped down beside her. "That question is easy to answer. That bastard of a man she married got to us both."

At his honesty, Nina's brows rose in surprise. With a slight smile he glanced up at her, shrugged his shoulders by way of explanation and then shook his head.

"I always fall hard for the tall, dark, handsome types. I guess the Comtesse did too, at the time," he sighed and sat up. With elbows on his knees he leaned forward as if to examine a spot on the carpeted floor.

"It was so long ago, I was brought over just a few years before the Comtesse arrived. At the time the Baron was not very discriminating, and he had an insatiable thirst for power. He felt there were two ways to gain power – by control and by wealth. For him, he procreated to his heart's delight for the control it gave him over his children, and that's how I was brought over. I was just one of his many dalliances. As for the Comtesse, what better way for the Baron to climb his way up the social order than to marry the daughter of a Comte? Comtesse Laurensa was his bargaining chip. Once he had her, he achieved the status he desired, or so we thought," Amadieu explained.

"He was not happy with the arrangement?" Nina found herself drawn into the tale of intrigue.

"No, hardly. With the title of 'Comte' he was going to move right up into the elite social order of France. Like he did with Comtesse Laurensa, he set a target on the rich and elite of Paris." His voice was steady and calm.

"And the Comtesse, what was to become of her?" Nina asked her friend.

"Oh, the Comte had it all planned. She was to be met with an untimely accident. He had it all planned out. After she retired to her coffin the human servants were to move her to the backyard. They had orders to open the lid at noon, and the rest would be history. The young Comtesse would be gone, and the

Comte would be a widower and free of any scandals. He would marry even higher within the social order," he explained.

"But that did not work?"

"Well, the problem was the Comte's plan is that he was very nasty to us servants. Oh yes, I had some fun with him, I must admit." A sly smile came to Amadieu's face, and then cleared up as he turned and gazed at Nina with a serious expression. "By this time the years had passed by and we here in the château watched history pass around us. While the Comte ignored it all as nonsense, we servants learned the lessons well, and the one thing that the Comte failed to understand from the social protests in Grenoble is that masters would only be masters as long as servants allowed them to be," he explained. "Word spread quickly through the servants' quarters of what he had planned to do, and none of us would have his plan succeed. So instead, the mortal workmen walked his coffin out to the open." He smiled wryly. "Oh, I hear tell that the Comte made the most ghastly of popping noises when the sun fell on him." He giggled hysterically.

"Amadieu, you did not?" Nina asked, a bit surprised by her friend's merriment.

"I did not do it myself, but in democratic fashion, I added my vote. After all, the Comtesse was always good to us servants. She saw us for who we were; she knew our names and treated us with respect. There was not a single person on staff who did not mourn the day that she died a mortal existence and began a new life as a vampire. We knew that it was being done against her will," Amadieu stated. At Nina's confused expression, he sighed theatrically and smiled down at her. "I can tell that I have much to teach you of liberty and freedom of choice. We all believe in this fervently and when the Baron, who had become a Comte through his marriage, turned his wife into a vampire, she had no free will. Yes, *Poupette*, it was a sad day when the Comtesse passed away." He shook his head and wiped at the moisture in his eyes.

"Then this is all true? It is not a dream. The Comtesse is a vampire? You are a vampire?" Nina asked with a hushed whisper.

"No, it is not a dream, and yes, we are vampires," Amadieu answered.

"How many more?" Amazement laced her question.

"Not many. Most moved on after Isabelle, that is, Isabelle, Baronne de la Chorange passed away. I believe it was too hard to be here amidst all the memories and sadness. Only a small handful of us, those loyal to the Comtesse, remained." Amadieu's voice held sorrow.

"Was the Baroness, was she also a vampire?" Nina asked.

"Oh Heavens, no! She was mortal through and through. I think if she had wanted to cross over, the Comtesse would have obliged. But again, free will. The Comtesse would never ask. It is not her way." The tall man leaned back and gazed up at the tiled ceiling.

Nina thought over his words. When the question remained on the tip of her tongue, she turned to her vampire friend. "How did the Baroness die?"

"An illness, a plague that took many good people. It raged through the land quickly. We thought we would be immune so far away from the larger cities, but it was not meant to be. First a few mortal servants died, then others. A few of the mortal servants asked to be turned into vampires, and they were brought over, safely away from the plagues of mortal man, free to live an eternity in the night," Amadieu explained as a thoughtful expression crossed his features.

"It was hard on the Comtesse. She sat beside the Baroness day and night, never once leaving her side. I know that she wanted to bring her over. Every fiber of her being was fighting the urge, but the Baroness was too far gone. She was too deep in the fever to even know to ask for it, and the Comtesse, she would never cross the line by bringing someone over who did not ask first. After all, it was done to her against her will, and she still remembered the anger and hatred toward that man who took that choice away. No, she is truly a gentle woman, and free will still means something in this château, even if it's only empty words elsewhere," he lamented.

"And now? What does she do? Why does she go to the attic so often when it brings her such pain?" Nina felt she already knew the answer, but waited for her friend's response.

"Because she is lonely, and she misses her lover. She and the Baroness were very close." Amadieu's eyes laid on her as if conveying a deep dark secret. "After the Baroness died, it was as if she died too, except with her, she is cursed with everlasting life," he finished solemnly.

"Nina found herself contemplating his words carefully. Even after he left, she paced the length of her room. Her hands traced the outline of the correspondence between the Comtesse and Baronne. She fought the eternal battle waging within her psyche.

Vampires were evil. Vampires were hideous creatures lurking through the shadows. Vampires preyed on the innocence of man. Vampires were hideous creatures to be searched out and destroyed. This is what she had learned from her many days of reading.

Yet the Comtesse, with all of the darkness forced upon her, had somehow managed to find goodness within. How could she be so vile and evil if she held such pure and sublime love for the Baronne de la Chorange? Through the rest of the night and all of the day these questions and more raged through Nina's adolescent mind.

When night fell, she half-expected Amadieu to arrive in her room for their usual night of talk. But he did not come. Instead, she woke from a slight slumber to find the door to her room opened. When she noticed the candles lit, she moved around the room, but there was no Amadieu. What she found were the bundles of letters neatly stacked with the ribbons secured around each corresponding bundle. On top of them lay a single note in a delicate script.

> *Poupette,*
> *She would have never allowed you to read these if she did not want you to.*
>
> > *Your humble friend,*
> > *Amadieu*

At his note, Nina's brow arched in surprise. She had never thought to wonder how, with such ease, she had found these letters. Nor did she even give it a second thought that so many pieces could be missing without their owner noticing. But now, as she read the letter from her friend, a thought dawned in her mind.

Like clockwork the soft, gentle weeping began to filter through the air. Nina listened to its soulful cry as she felt her heart rapidly skipping beats. She felt her tongue cross over dry lips as she gazed down, once more, at the bundles on the table.

"She would never ask it, not for herself," Nina whispered out loud as realization set in.

Standing alone in her room Nina heard the still, small voice in the back of her mind confirming what Amadieu had tried to tell her. No, the Comtesse would never burden herself upon another. If the opportunity to find another mate occurred, she would not be the first to take the necessary steps.

Nina found herself moving on instinct. She dropped Amadieu's letter where she stood and made her way from the room. The journey that seemed to take an eternity before now seemed an easy jaunt. When she stood at the bottom of the staircase leading to the attic, she wasted little time in cinching up her skirt hem and climbing the steps. Without a candle or lantern one would have used more caution, but she did not care. Nina was beyond caution and beyond caring. Having traveled this path so many times by day, she took firm, strong steps until she stood behind the figure sitting before the large oil painting. The cries of sorrow and pain rang through the attic and pierced Nina's heart.

True to her dark nature, the Comtesse grew deathly silent for only a moment. Then, like a vicious storm suddenly descending, the tall woman stood before Nina. Her eyes were ablaze with the red anger of Hell. Her body began transforming into the hideous beast before Nina's eyes.

"I told you!" the creature of sorrow, pain and despair began to shout.

Nina stood her ground. She looked up at the unholy beast, her own eyes brimming with tears as she felt the fear racing through her. With a single shake of her head, she sighed as a tear tumbled uncontrollable down her cheek.

"No. I will not obey!" Nina heard her voice speak out with a boldness she did not know she had.

The creature stood before her in silence. It appeared confused or perhaps moved by the strength and conviction in Nina's words. When it seemed as if time stood still, the form of the beast metamorphosed before her eyes, and the Comtesse stood, once more, looking down upon her. Testing Nina's sincerity, the Lady stared down into her eyes, holding her captive with her hypnotic vampiric magic. Then, like a child suddenly lost, the Comtesse fell to her knees before Nina. Arms filled with inhuman strength wrapped around her waist and held on for dear life as she wept uncontrollably in the folds of Nina's skirts.

"There, there," Nina cooed as she ran her fingers through

the Comtesse's long, silky hair. "You need not mourn alone; you need not ever be alone again. 'Intreat me not to leave thee, or to return from following after thee: for whither thou goest, I will go; and where thou lodgest, I will lodge: thy people shall be my people.'" Nina's words held the truth and sincerity of heart. The Comtesse only wept louder for the years of solitude and despair she had experienced. In this single moment, the veil of sorrow began to lift from a heart so long in mourning.

27 March, evening – Diary of Mademoiselle Cecilia Natashia Dupuin

By the Blessed Mother everything I have written of the account of Madame Faivre is true! I scarcely believed it myself as I was transcribing all of her words, but I swear by all that is holy this tale is not a work of fancy in an old lady's mind. It is true and this is how I know.

As she finished her tale, a sound at the door was heard. The nurse rose when a tall figure walked into the room, and there, before my very eyes, stood the figure of the Comtesse herself. She is just as painted in the canvas that hangs downstairs. Her dark, flowing hair fell past strong broad shoulders. Her eyes, may God pardon me, her eyes are the most beautiful shade of grey I have ever seen. But she is also different from her portrait. Instead of a grand ballroom dress, she wore the clothing of a man. She wore a vest over a neatly pressed shirt, and her tapered trousers were tucked into high black riding boots. It was then I realized where I had seen her before.

This was the person who had gently carried Madame Faivre from the château when she took leave to go to Geneva. How could I have missed it? Surely I should have noticed that the figure was a woman, but how could I have guessed? Would a gentle woman have the strength to carry another, even a frail old lady?

I then answered my own questions. Yes, because the Comtesse is no ordinary woman. She is a vampire with vampiric strength, just as was told to me from Madame Faivre's dictation.

I could not help but stop what I was doing as the woman entered the room, and I worried that my presence was not welcomed. As I rose to give them privacy, Madame Faivre took hold of my hand and held me steady. Her eyes beseeched mine as a gentle smile crossed her lips. With a shaky hand, she reached out to me, her warm withered fingers clasping my hand.

"There is more for you to do." Madame Faivre's voice rang with a pleasant tone.

"Madame?" Filled with confusion, I looked from her to the elegant woman.

"It is time for you to tell her story. You must hear what my beloved has to say," she spoke gently, turning her gaze to the Comtesse. "You will do this for me, yes?" Madame Faivre asked her vampire lover.

"Anything," came the woman's solemn promise as she took my employer's hand in her own.

"Very well then," Madame Faivre released a sigh of relief as she lay back upon her pillow, her eyes gazing lovingly at the vampire Comtesse.

It was then that I nodded and quietly left the room, allowing the two the privacy that they needed. I do not know what my new job will entail but I am certain it shall be as spiritually rewarding as my sessions with Madame Faivre have been. Perhaps in due course more will be revealed to me about this mysterious château, the people who dwell within, and the Comtesse herself.

Part 2

Chapter 4

28 March, evening – Diary of Mademoiselle Cecilia Natashia Dupuin

The Comtesse Laurensa Catherin de la Fontaine wasted little time to informing me of my upcoming duties. It appears as if by mutual agreement, I am no longer Madame Faivre's employee but now belong to the Comtesse. Were I not intrigued I might be offended by the quick handoff I received.

I cannot fault Madame Faivre, for she is very old and weak. I wonder if she truly felt finished with her dictation, or did she fall ill? Perhaps one might never know. And what of my new duties? I look back through my memory of the studies from Madame Ségolène's school, and do not recollect there ever being a course covering this topic. Not only to meet a real vampire, but also to transcribe her words for posterity is something I doubt has ever been done or something likely ever to be done again. For whom, but I, would be foolish enough to court danger in this way? The fact I shall be transcribing for a vampire should give credence to disbelievers who think vampires as mere creatures of fables. Or perhaps they will think me mad?

I can only wonder what designs are in store for me. Are vampires as blood thirsty as described in those forbidden novels? What will become of me when this tale is complete? Am I like Scheherazade who must bide my time and extend my life with each passing story? If so, how much longer will the stories last?

No, I cannot allow my mind to wander like this. Since arriving at Madame Faivre's, I have received nothing but kindness and hospitality. Yes, it is true that the doors were locked upon me, and I was kept a virtual prisoner by night. However, now fully aware of the dangers around me, I can see that it was done for my safety. Knowing my circumstances, I no longer hear the telltale sounds of Amadieu locking my door. Although I have been given my freedom, I find myself cautious and respectful of the privacy of those who dwell in this château.

After learning the truth about this mysterious place, I know vampires actually exist and many live within these walls. I now recognize their appearance. Amadieu's pale countenance is reflected in the servants who work at night. The coach driver, hardly ever seen, moves about the land freely at night. Maids who busy themselves through the château at night are never seen in the daylight. How queer to have had them walking around me, yet I never noticed them before. Now it all makes sense to this country bumpkin of a girl.

So I shall settle down to transcribe the words of a vampire. Rather than speaking to me in the main family room that Madame Faivre and I frequented, the vampire has requested that I attend to her in her private office. Imagine, a vampire who keeps a private office. How strange it all seems to me. My rational mind speaks to me of the absurdity of it all. After all, how many vampires would actually wish to have their lives documented for posterity? Methinks not many, if any at all.

I hear the knock upon my door as Amadieu informs me that the Comtesse is ready. While I was working for Madame Faivre by day, I now find myself employed by her vampire companion, the Comtesse, in the evening. I hope I do not fall asleep from fatigue while she dictates her words to me.

28 March, evening – The recollections of Comtesse Laurensa Catherine de la Fontaine

"You must find this whole thing rather strange, yes?" the Comtesse questioned in a strong and clear voice.

She stood at the large open window staring out at the pitch black darkness. Her back remained to me. Like before, she wore the garb of a man. The dark trousers tapered over her womanly hips, and the grey silk vest accentuated her long sleeved white shirt. Long, dark tresses fell over her shoulders and by the light of the lamps, it held a healthy sheen. When the vampire turned, I found myself momentarily mesmerized by her piercing grey eyes.

"Do you know how many of you girls have come to our château?" the Comtesse asked. When I gave a negative shake of my head, the vampire smiled as she moved to sit in a high-backed chair, ignoring the one situated nearby behind a large rosewood desk. In an easy, fluid move the stately woman lounged with a leg delicately crossed as she began to gaze into the flames of the fireplace. "There have been a total of three girls; you are the fourth," she informed me.

"None have made it this far. The first one, a little pup who never should have been let out in public, was so fearful of the château she refused to come down the first morning. By the time they got her from her room, Amadieu had to take her to the chapel in Grenoble where he hired a Sister to transport the *petite fille* to the convent of Rouvray-Catillon. The second one made it as far as a week before she tried to seduce Amadieu. It seems she had other things on her mind." The Comtesse released a tired sigh. "The third, let us just say that once she laid eyes upon me, she was not good for anyone, least of all herself." She shook her head in displeasure.

"Tell me, Mademoiselle Dupuin, are you not frightened?"

I answered as honestly as I could. "No, Comtesse Laurensa Catherine de la Fontaine."

"Please, let us dispense with such a long name." The vampire waved her hand in a movement similar to Madame Faivre. "You may call me Comtesse until I inform you otherwise."

"Yes, Comtesse," I replied.

"You should take it as a compliment that you have come this far," she stated as she leaned back, her eyes turning once more from me.

"May I ask, Comtesse, why am I the fourth? Why has Madame Faivre retained so many girls to transcribe her words?" I asked, leaning forward a bit.

"You may ask." The Comtesse seemed almost bored, her eyes moving from the flames of the fires to me. "You are here to transcribe Madame Faivre's life for when she moves on."

I gasped covering my mouth with my hand, aghast at the very idea of the dear woman's demise. "Oh, my. She is ill?" I felt the tears tugging at my heart as my eyes grew suddenly moist.

"If she is ill, this is the fourth time." The Comtesse waved away my concern. "You see, as of the past decade, Madame Faivre has taken to the notion that she has one foot in the grave. She believes she is on a mission, but I tell you now, she is as full of life as you or…" She did not finish her words, instead looked away as if realizing a great faux pas almost occurred.

"The Madame is frequently on her death bed. Each time she cleaves to death, we must send for a new graduated girl. Once the girls does not work out, then Madame rises from her death bed to begin anew," the Comtesse explained.

"Then she is not ill?" I asked.

"No," came the curt reply, before turning to look directly at me. Under such a piercing gaze, I had to avert my eyes. When this seemed futile I looked around her office and noted the bookshelves nearby, the nondescript paintings, and a door on the far wall. I began to wonder what might possibly be behind such a mysterious door. Perhaps a secret room? An enclave where the vampire's coffin was kept?

"You think too much," she stated coldly, gazing at me with contempt. "I suppose you want me to show you what lies behind that door?"

I remained silent and averted my eyes to my steno pad.

"Very well. You choose to curb your curiosity wisely, for very few enter that room," she warned sternly.

"Y-Yes, Madame, umm, Comtesse," I blurted out as I kept my gaze focused on my lap where my pen hovered precariously over my notepad, eagerly awaiting its first stroke against the paper.

Silence filled the room, somewhere down the hall the sound of a clock ticked away.

"I suppose you want to hear my story now, to get my life down on script?" the Comtesse finally said with a tired voice. "I know you wish to know about the Baronne de la Chorange, yes?" she asked, her gaze resting upon me more tenderly, and I quickly nodded assent.

"Well, you can get that notion out of your head. My memories of the Baronne are mine alone," the Comtesse snapped as her gaze turned fierce again. For one heart pounding minute we looked at each other until I lowered my eyes in respect. After a moment of silence, the Comtesse began to speak again.

"You are the fourth girl here, the only one who has made it this far, and I suppose you wish to know about Nin...Madame Faivre, yes?" she asked me.

"I will transcribe whatever you wish me to, Comtesse." I held my voice even and steady as I glanced into her eyes. She seemed to be examining me and then, with a release of a sigh, she lowered her gaze to the folded hands on her lap.

"I imagine there is no clear way to begin without some mention of the Baronne," the Comtesse relented.

"Isabelle, Baronne de la Chorange," the vampire stated with strength. Then, with a slight whisper, she said the woman's name again with a tone of lament. "I have not said her name for some time. I have not spoken about her, not even to my beloved. But now I say her name with all the want that is in my soul. Isabelle, my Baronne. She was my everything, and when she died..." The Comtesse grew silent as if contemplating her words.

"Everything changed after she was gone. Everything." A soft tone registered the melancholy of the vampire as she began to tell her tale that had happened so long ago...

*****

The days and nights passed like a blur for the vampire, and still she did not feed regularly. The château, once filled with life, laughter, and happiness, had grown dark and silent over the passing years. The pristine hallways grew dark and dingy. Cobwebs formed over the open doorways and windows. The white Italian marble was covered with a layer of dirt, but still the Comtesse paid it no mind.

Back when life was grand and there was not a care in the world, Comtesse Laurensa thought she had found happiness. The once brooding melancholy consuming her was vanquished by the presence of a single woman. They had twenty years together, a short span in a vampire's life, and then everything changed.

Laurensa watched helplessly as, one by one, the unseen fiend claimed the human inhabitants of her château. She had heard of plagues hitting other countries, Italy, Switzerland, Germany, and then it was in Paris. She wrongly thought that, as long as they remained away from the crowded cities, all would be well. But it was not. In due course she witnessed the invisible monster making its way throughout her household. Many of the mortal servants either perished, or were turned into creatures of the night by their own request. Each time someone asked for it, a part of Laurensa's frozen heart screamed out in protest. She, more than anyone, knew the agony living a cursed life could be. In the end, it was their choice, their decision to make.

Laurensa had never asked for this unholy life. If she had known what was to come, she would have run as far away from her family as she could. She would have joined a convent rather than be forced into marriage with a hellish creature. Life in poverty as an unknown was better than existing in this state. She had not run away and, therefore, met the fate of many before her. Unlike them, she was not merely a bride, a wife to bear fruit for the master of the château. No, her master and husband felt it fit to turn her into the same fiend as he. Ever since becoming a vampire, food had no taste and wine gave no comfort. Once she was turned by that jackal of a man, all she cared about, all she longed for, was the taste of warm blood. This, more than anything, disgusted her.

This internal disgust was a throwback to her mortal days, her husband told her. Laurensa did not know, nor did she care. All she knew was that the taking of life, especially innocent life, dug at the very fibers of her being. Yet what was she to do? The moral imperative of her new psyche demanded she kill to survive. But was this the only way?

Her husband looked down upon mortals. He scoffed at their very existence, yet what he yearned for so much was to be a part of those short-lived creatures' lives. He wanted their acceptance and respect. Most importantly, he wanted the rank to make every mortal bow before him. This is why he married Laurensa. Once their marriage was sealed, he moved up in rank to comte. However, she never granted him the courtesy the title gave him. No, to her, he would always be of lower rank than she. He would always be nothing more than a jackal from Hell.

His rise in status did not last long. In the end when it seemed that her husband had grown tired of her, he decided to dispose of her as easily as he disposed of the mortals he drained. It was at this time Laurensa realized his bringing her over to this existence did not make him the authority on how a vampire should live. Once the servants dispatched him, she was able to set out alone in life. After a short time of bumbling her way through undead life, she quickly learned of other ways to survive.

True, in the height of bloodlust there was sometimes things she could not control. With a strength greater than a mortal woman or man, she was able to quickly take over, rule, and dispense of her prey. But she did not enjoy this. Only after the death of her husband did she learn how to control the bloodlust. By moving about at night, taking a little here, a little there, Laurensa kept from being pulled into the deepest despair of the fires from Hell.

On this night she felt the inexorable tugging of her nature. She knew if she did not do something tonight, the lust would soon consume her, and she might find herself murdering an innocent mortal. Rather than succumb to her baser needs, she went out to quench her thirst.

While Laurensa stood under the rays of the full moon she glanced up at the guardian above the crypt. Seemingly knowing she was a demon of Hell, its cold, white eyes followed her every move. She felt its bitter hatred as it stood silent watch over the Baronne's crypt. Even after so many years, it still stood silent vigil. Like the guardian, the semicircle of marble angels also watched her every move.

Laurensa was not a religious person, yet when she commissioned the artist to create the pieces for her beloved's final resting place, she never knew of the magic that would be instilled within them. Many of the statues have since been replicated and sit throughout the world, but she knew that she held the originals. As the Angel of Grief sat up from its weeping position, the marble statue watched her like a sentinel. Its ever-present gaze remained alert, expecting her to defile the crypt of her long dead lover.

With a tired sigh, the Comtesse knelt down and swept the old, dying flowers away from the marble marker and replaced them with the bouquet of new spring flowers. When she rested her palm against the marble, she thought she felt a resounding spark of life filtering through her fingertips. Before hope could rise, she released an inward growl and shook her head at her own stupid wistfulness.

Mortals did not live for eternity. This trait was reserved for vampires alone. Knowing this did not make it any easier for her to continue through life all alone, save the few immortal servants who chose to remain faithfully by her side. Angered by the futility of her existence, she rose from her place and looked toward the pitch black crypt. With her vampire eyes she saw into the darkness and knew behind the marble wall rested a wooden coffin. Within the coffin were the remains of her beloved. After so many years, the Baronne would be reduced to leathered skin. Her fine velvet and silk garments would crackle and break with age.

No, this is not how Laurensa wanted to remember her beloved. Instead, she would remember the days of laughter and merriment. The softly intoned words of love, this is what she would remember. Every time she looked into the crypt, she would not think of the empty body that lay within, but instead would remember the warm, mortal flesh that once rested in her embrace.

At her melancholy thoughts Laurensa rose to her full height. She pulled the light cape closer around her shoulders and then turned away from the crypt. As she walked out of the cemetery she felt the immobile eyes of the statues follow her closely. When she moved to the rear of the château, she knew if she turned around, the marble statues would be back in their original positions. The one high atop the crypt would be sprawled over the archway, its wings folded out and around itself as it wept for all of eternity, while the others in the semicircle gazed down upon the mourning angel. Laurensa did not turn around to look. Instead, she took the initial steps needed. With eyes closed she felt the magic of her unholy powers fill her soul until she became weightless.

In the night no one would see how easily they moved between bodies. Those who did not know of or believe in vampires would be hard pressed to even see the change from human to animal form. Once the cape closed around her, the transformation was complete and she began her flight. Her flapping wings carried her higher into the sky. When she opened her eyes she saw the distorting image of her black beak. Her eyes no longer saw in front of her, but to the side as any bird of prey.

Her husband had liked to take the form of a bat. He thrived on the fear he caused in the mortals. Laurensa was not like him. Instead, she liked to feel the strong talons of a falcon. The strong wings cut cleanly through the wind and allowed her to fly even farther than most vampires. Now, with the thirst coming upon her, she knew exactly where to find the liquid to quench her desires.

With an arch of her feathered head, Laurensa allowed an updraft to pick her up and lift her higher into the darkness. Some time later, she released a screech and tilted her wings to begin her descent. As she grew closer to the earth she recognized the familiar hamlet. Almost two days away from Genoble, and more than a week away from her château, the distance kept her people from harm. If she were ever caught, killed or captured, they could not trace her origins to her servants who remained behind.

As she swooped down she noticed the darkness over the rooftops. Everyone was safely tucked away in their beds, their doors barred from within. On this night, many would continue to sleep snuggled in their peaceful dreams. Only a few might be restless, but for them it would be like a fleeting memory. Those she used hardly remembered her nightly visits as anything other than a pleasant dream, or ethereal visit.

With a controlled movement, the falcon that was her body soared over the rooftops until she came to the window she desired. When she moved closer she felt her magical powers slowly transforming her to the shape she once held as a mortal. Only when she landed silently on the cobblestone did her full, womanly body emerge from the wings.

Laurensa remained silent and listened with her acute vampire senses. If she concentrated hard enough, she could hear the soft murmurs of those sleeping nearby. When the hunger pangs reminded her of her quest, she turned her attention to the farthest home. Just as she was in flight, she moved silently to the abode. Concealed in darkness, the windows were barred on the first floor. When she glanced up she noticed the second floor window open almost as if someone inside was expecting her. With a rueful smile, Laurensa pushed her cape over her shoulders and moved to the wall. In a slow, steady stride, she clasped her palms against the rocky structure and began pulling herself up along the wall. Her vampire abilities allowed her to climb the side of the building as easily as a lizard climbed a boulder.

Ever since the death of her husband, Laurensa took to dressing in men's clothing. With her new emancipation, she declared that wearing dresses was a cruel punishment, even for a vampire. Neither the mortal nor immortal servants raised any objection when she took all of her husband's clothing and had them tailored to her body. Eventually she began to wear custom made men's clothing from some of the finest tailors in Europe. Now as she climbed the wall she was grateful for her decision because, while the frilliness of women's clothing might catch a man's attention, it did little in aiding vampires in their exploits. As for her clothing, Amadieu made no excuses for taking all of her dresses and having them tapered to his body. On days when he felt like laughing, he would even prance around her fully dressed in one of her gowns.

Upon reaching the open window Laurensa smiled to herself as she entered the dark room. She had no need to ask for permission to enter, because it had been given many moons ago. Once in the darkness, she glanced around the familiar setting. She closed her eyes and felt the sweet mortal who slept innocently in the bed. Pleased by this sensation, she moved closer. As she reached out and barred the single door with her magical vampire powers, she unclasped her cape and let it drop to the floor.

"Am I alone?" a soft, feminine voice whispered in the darkness.

"Do you wish to be?" Laurensa asked as she stood over the bed.

In answer to her question, the mortal woman lifted the coverlet invitingly.

Laurensa always knew that she was different. Even when she was a mortal, she always knew that part of her was unlike other women. Only when she became a vampire and left behind her mortal life did she understand her true nature. In the beginning her husband used to watch her with her kills. He used to take delight in the ecstasy she brought her prey. When she killed them, he would eagerly move forward and partake of her kill and then, like a rutting beast, would mount her and expend what little energy he had left upon her flesh. The latter part Laurensa never enjoyed. No matter how many times he had sex with her, she could never fully enjoy it as she did with women.

Laurensa did not care for those days. She preferred the way it was now, alone in the darkness with only herself and the young mortal woman. The name of prey did not matter because for a vampire names were fleeting. But Laurensa knew each of the women of whom she partook. She knew their scent, touch, and taste. She bathed herself in their essence, and in return, she gave them the most enticing experience within her power. This time was no different.

Without ado, she moved to the young woman. This creature was not a girl, yet not a woman. The daughter of a protestant minister, this girl was sheltered and kept away from the world. She did not know about the dangers lurking in the darkness. In every way, her parents had kept her pure and innocent, and this is what Laurensa preferred. She had taken this innocent creature for almost a year and had showered upon the girl the pleasure of love. If she was to be married off to a man, Laurensa decided that she would allow the minister's daughter to feel all of the glories a body could experience.

Laurensa felt the young woman's hand on her shoulders. Like a starved woman, she pulled and tugged on her garments until they were discarded one after another. As if she held her own magic, the mortal's nightgown was suddenly gone, thrown upon the wooden floor with Laurensa's clothing.

"It has been months, my night lover," the minister's daughter whispered as she began to kiss along Laurensa's neck.

"You know I could not leave you for long." Laurensa felt her voice grow husky as their bodies rubbing against each other.

There was nothing as sweet as a soft, warm body. Nothing pleased the Comtesse as much as a pliant, willing lover. The softness of a woman, her sweet intoxicating scent was enough to spur Laurensa's needs. On this night she would be gentle, yet not linger long in foreplay. Instead she kissed her lover deeply. As her mouth rained kisses over the mortal flesh, she inhaled the pleasant scent of life.

Just as she did before, Laurensa used her unholy web of magic and cast it over this mortal. She felt the woman's needs and heard her whispered thoughts. The baser needs, the primordial desires of her prey, flooded Laurensa in a wave of ecstasy, and she relished every moment of it. As a way of appeasing the young woman's lust, Laurensa complied with all of her demands.

Arms and legs entwined. Cold, immortal flesh rubbed against the warm woman. Fingers once gentle became urgent as they sought out their treasure. A cold, wistful tongue once locked in a kiss now dove lower, searching until the mortal woman gave what the vampire desired.

Time seemed endless as they moved in unison. Laurensa heard the woman's whispered pleas. She knew the heightened pleasure because it was her own. Each stroke of her tongue, each probe of her fingers brought the minster's daughter closer to the brink. The young woman squirmed uncontrollably as low, meowing sounds escaped her throat. Only after the woman gave herself completely did Laurensa turn her attention to her own needs.

Filled with the hunger, the Comtesse moved up the long body until she covered her completely. Warm, human legs wrapped around her torso as gentle arms circled her chest. Their soft, pliant bosoms molded against each other and for a moment, the vampire could feel the mortal's erratic heartbeat through this connection. Knowing what was to come next, the minister's daughter smiled in the darkness as she turned her head away, baring her neck.

Yes, the vampire required blood to survive. But she had learned over the years that her survival did not require the taking of life. With this knowledge, she chose her willing victims wisely. In the darkness she felt the change come over her. Her eyes, once placid, burned red and a growl escaped her control. The mortal's body arched enticingly below her, her hips pushing upward like a gentle rolling sea as if beckoning the inevitable crescendo of their union. Obligingly, Laurensa lowered herself as her sharp canine teeth met their target. Whatever pain the mortal might have felt, the vampire's power took away. The piercing of flesh was momentary and then the blood began to flow.

In mortal life the Comtesse had tasted the finest wines of the land. She knew the nuances of each one and could tell the origin of each grape. As a human, she loved the tangy sweetness of wine. But now, as an immortal, nothing tasted as sweet against her lips as the tangy blood of an innocent.

Laurensa knew when to stop. When she was deep in the bloodlust, without conscious knowledge and acting on instinct, she left the humans just moments from death. Sometimes she watched their life leave their eyes. But she was not that same person. She was not drowning in her bloodlust any longer. The Comtesse was in control and when she had taken what was needed, she stopped and covered the open wounds with her tongue. Even this simple courtesy caused the insatiable girl to whine and beg for more, but Laurensa did not comply.

Instead she closed the girl's wounds with her saliva, then, in a soft suggestive voice, whispered close to the minister's daughter's ear, "You are a little minx, but you are tired." Her breath caused the girl to wiggle uncontrollably even as her eyes began to close.

"When?" the young woman begged.

"When I hunger for you again," the Comtesse answered as she rose from the girl's naked body. As she looked down at the young woman, she smiled when she saw the pale form fall deeply into sleep. Her ample bosoms rose with each soft breath she took. By the pale moonlight, Laurensa softly ran her fingers over the pink, round nipples, and then moved reluctantly from the bed.

As the minister's daughter slept peacefully after her exertion, Laurensa quickly dressed. When she pulled her cape around her shoulders, she turned to the door and released her magical control over it. If the minister and his wife had heard anything, they would simply think their child dreamt of her future husband. They would smile at each other with the thought that soon after her marriage, they would be grandparent. No one would ever know that a vampire had been the cause of the girl's nocturnal delights.

When Laurensa moved to the open window, she looked back at the sleeping girl as a satisfied smile curled her lips. Daylight would not be upon them for some time, and in that time she would be able to pay a visit to two other women. By the time her night visits were finished, she would have had enough blood to sate her for many days. When the bloodlust began again, she would move on to another hamlet and another set of sweet, young girls. If nothing else, she would give them a taste of true pleasure before they were wedded off to young men.

29 March, morning – Diary of Mademoiselle Cecilia Natashia Dupuin

I can scarcely grasp all that was told to me, but as I reread the words of the Comtesse, I have to believe my ears were not deceiving me. I did my best to concentrate on my task, but her words were so captivating, so alluring, I found myself mesmerized by the very nature of her descriptions. Partway through the dictation I realized I had stopped scribing and was staring intently at the Comtesse's pale form. Although I had previously noticed a strangely appealing nature to the woman, I now saw, for the first time, how truly beautiful she is. Were I to say that the oil canvas did her little justice, it would not be a lie, for she is far more attractive than any woman I have ever before met. Her long, dark hair held a sheen which glimmered with sparkles in the dim lamp lights. Pale skin covered finely chiseled cheek bones. Her nose was as perfect as her rosy red lips and her pale grey eyes seemed to peer into my soul.

I was shocked out of my trance by the sudden silence in the room. When I realized that her gaze remained upon me,

I jumped slightly and glanced down at my steno pad. In an unconscious move I wiped the sheen of perspiration from my upper lip as I returned my attention to the task for which I was hired. Seemingly amused by my befuddlement, the Comtesse chuckled softly. Her eyes grew to slits as a smile crossed her lips. Without another word, she resumed the narration of her seduction of various women, and I continued to scribe every word she spoke.

I honestly do not know if I can continue with my task, for it is hard to listen to such a sweetly melodic voice explain the art of seduction. Although I have never lain with another, man or woman, I find my curiosity mounting. Yes, my bosom friend Margarie and I had a few encounters, some gentle hugs, perhaps a caress here and there, childish explorations, but we had never shared what the Comtesse explained. Now she has me intrigued with possibilities.

I cannot allow my wandering dreams to interfere with my professionalism. I cannot allow childish thoughts to enter into my mind because I must complete the job I am assigned. Perhaps, when this task is over and I return to Paris, I might encounter another like me who would be amiable to such a liaison. Until then I must be focused no matter how intoxicating the Comtesse might be.

Chapter 5

29 March, evening – Diary of Mademoiselle Cecilia Natashia Dupuin

I did not realize the difficulty I would have in sleeping by day and working at night. Amadieu was kind enough to have the shutters on the windows of my room barred and the drapes drawn shut. Once the lamps were dimmed, it appeared as if it were night.

Although I fought to stay awake during the night, once I was in my room my body recoiled at this change and I found sleep hard to come by. Each time I felt myself drifting I began to see unusual images play out before my eyes -- images of the Comtesse's gentle touch upon bare flesh. Sounds floating magically within the air filled my dreams, and I woke several times. Each time I noted the hour and realized that I had slept but a short time.

How do vampires keep such hours, I wonder? How are they able to retire during the day and wake all through the night? But then, they are queer creatures, are they not? They are of the night, born into a life where they must live in shadows for all of eternity. I wonder how the Comtesse managed to survive for so long. True, she has her servants for companionship, but is it enough? Is going from château to château the ideal manner for one's constitution? It certainly enabled the Comtesse the ability to survive while also maintaining her respect for human life.

How strange a vampire she is. In all of my studies at Madame Ségolène's school, I have never read a novel where a vampire preferred to avoid taking life. Often they are described as bloodthirsty fiends with an appetite to kill. In all of these books, vampires are creatures who are seen preying upon humans with a vengeance, and now I learn they do not, in fact, enjoy killing. They do not long for the death of us mere mortals. At least, one of them does not. The Comtesse, like her companion Madame Faivre, has demonstrated nothing but kindness. Even Amadieu, their servant who is also a vampire, appears to be a kind gentle soul. Who would ever believe this? Certainly I would not should anyone have tried to tell me this a few months ago. But now that I am here and have been privy to their words, I know it to be true. These vampires are not like the ones we have read about, and I wonder why this is so. Perhaps this is a subject I shall have to ponder further.

Could it be that there are others like these vampires? Perhaps the stories are merely works of fancy to frighten the feeble-hearted? I know I felt great terror upon reading such novels. If I had been told before arriving of where I was to be employed, I might never have agreed to this position. "Better to be a pauper begging on the streets," I might have said. How unfortunate it would have been for me to not have experienced this little adventure.

Despite all that has transpired, I find myself wondering if the Comtesse was always this way? Was she always a gentle soul who despised the taking of human life? She did mention that she once was like her husband casually taking human lives, but he prompted her to be so vile. Now that he is gone – and thank goodness for it – her calm, gentle soul seems to have flourished once again. How miraculous it is that she found another way to survive. Those innocent girls were none the worse for wear, and it seems, if anything, they received a great deal of pleasure in the Comtesse's company.

As I think of this I feel a heat crossing my cheeks and warmth building between my legs. I must remember to keep these wandering thoughts under control lest the Comtesse see the blush upon my cheeks. She would surely know the wanton and lascivious thoughts that cross my mind. If she knew perhaps she would tell Madame Faivre and whatever respect I have cultivated will be lost. I would be doomed to leave the château in shame.

No, I must keep my wandering thoughts in check and perform my duties. I am here to transcribe, and this is what I shall do. Whatever provocations the Comtesse's words elicit, I shall keep them to myself. No one will know my thoughts for fear I should be branded with a scandalous reputation. It is for me alone to know how I wonder about the Comtesse's cold, gentle touches.

Tonight she wishes to continue with her dictation. Upon leaving her office this morning she asked that I rest, for tonight she would reveal the darker side of her true nature. I do not know why, but when she first spoke of it I felt a sudden fear. It was as if the thought of being left alone with a primordial beast was too great to bear. But after a day of contemplation, I know whatever she might say holds no bearing upon my fondness for her and Madame Faivre. They will always be dear to me, and I shall always think of them with kindness.

29 March, evening – The recollections of Comtesse Laurensa Catherine de la Fontaine

"Am I as entertaining as Madame Faivre?" the Comtesse asked in an accusing voice. "I never wished to have my life transcribed and placed upon sheets of paper for posterity, but she has requested it. There is nothing I would refuse her." The Comtesse's candor was surprising. "If truth be told, I doubt these words shall ever reach outside my château," she added.

She stood at the window with her back to the room, just as she had the night before. Her gaze peered into the darkness as if searching for or watching something intently. Her long, dark hair cascaded past her broad shoulders almost to her waist. The man's suit she wore was tailored to enhance her womanly shape. When I sat in the assigned chair, the Comtesse turned and looked at me.

"You understand the relationship that Madame Faivre and I have, yes?" she asked me point blank. Feeling the warmth rise to my cheeks, I gazed into her intense grey eyes. With a slight smile, the woman broke the contact as she moved to sit in the high-backed chair. She moved with graceful, cat-like ease. "Yes, I do believe that you understand far more than you let on," she mused.

"Comtesse?" My voice was weak under the accusation.

The Comtesse examined me closely. Her full, pouting lips remained in a frown as her gaze peered into the depths of my soul. Before me her normally grey eyes turned indigo, then sapphire, and finally blood red. I felt as if my very essence was being touched by the hand of evil, but then it withdrew. Satisfied, she released a slight tsking sound as she leaned back in the chair. Her eyes closed as a tired sigh escaped.

"Things are so easy for the young," the Comtesse lamented as she closed her eyes for only a moment. When it appeared that the fatigue would not linger, the pale woman glanced directly at me.

"My previous words were... enticing, yes?" she asked me candidly.

I lowered my gaze in shame knowing my cheeks had turned a shade of deep crimson as I blushed. Sensing my embarrassment, she chortled before turning her eyes to the flames in the fireplace.

"No doubt you found my narration informative and... titillating." Her sultry voice seemed to sing. "Mark my words, Mademoiselle; things are not always as they appear. Once, I, too, was a fiend. Oh yes, do not look at me with such surprise. I assure you, I was as heinous as my dead husband," she explained. "Once, before I ever met Madame Faivre, I had lost my way. I was ruthless and unkind and did not care what I did or who I hurt. Sometimes, my actions were warranted, but other times..." her voice drifted with regret. "There were times when I thought I never could survive such an endless ordeal after the loss of the Baronne, but I did. As bleak and hopeless as it all seemed, the instinct to survive is very strong." The Comtesse's voice softened as she began relating her experiences from days long past...

*****

Laurensa did not know how many lonely days and nights had passed. She only knew that her life no longer held meaning. Once she had a reason to wake at night, to rise with the stars and move about freely. There was a time when laughter spilled easily from her lips, but that was many years ago. Now, all she could do was pass away the monotonous days waiting for the time when her end came or when she found the fortitude to go through with her desire to bathe in the morning sun one last time.

Laurensa was lonely, and although she did not realize it, she was deep in the midst of grieving. The few vampire staff who chose to remain loyal to her, watched her slow decline but were powerless to stop it. All they could do was make certain she did not dwell too deeply in her misery.

"Comtesse, what you need is a good, hearty meal," Amadieu, her valet, said as he helped her dress. Even the simple act of dressing had become tiresome to her.

"It is not that, Amadieu." Laurensa sighed as she sat wearily upon the divan. "I have partaken of nourishment already."

"No, you've only quenched your thirst, Comtesse. I am talking about going out and consuming until you belly is full. I am talking about feeling the pure animal drive well up within you until you see red."

Laurensa glanced up at Amadieu with a dejected expression on her face. She had heard him say this time and again. The animal impulse within had not been lost, and what she did, the partaking here and there of willing victims, only slaked her thirst. But Laurensa did not know if she could muster the strength needed to fell another victim, even if she found the desire to do so.

"Comtesse, I hear tell of a banker in Chambery, and evil man, an ogre, if one is to believe in those. He is vile to his workers and beats his wife severely. Why, there are even whispers of some impropriety with the finances," Amadieu's voice whispered conspiratorially even though they were alone. She looked back at him with a questioning arch of a brow. "Oh yes, he is evil, Comtesse, and if anyone is deserving..." The young vampire's voice drifted off.

"So this is how I should sate this thirst of mine, and all will be well?" Her voice sounded hollow in the room.

"All I am suggesting is that the sun will be setting soon. You will have ample time to go there and return before sunrise. Go to Chambery, find the banker, Boileau. Once you watch him, you'll know if he is deserving of life or death," Amadieu commented matter-of-factly and turned his attention to placing the black coat on his mistress. She was deep in thought as he continued, "If he is not suitable, then there are many young maidens there who would quench your thirst for yet another night."

"Perhaps," she whispered as she rose from her seat and began buttoning her coat closed. "Perhaps you are right. It has been a long time."

"Yes, too long. Now you go out, and we'll watch everything here." He gave a toothy smile.

"And for the rest of you?" she asked.

"Oh, we'll be fine. We'll probably just stay here. I hear there is a storm brewing, and I personally prefer to be indoors during such occasions," he explained as he took her cape from a hook and held it open for her.

"Boileau," she said the man's name as if putting it to memory.

"Yes, truly evil. Trust me he would not be missed by either his employees or family," Amadieu said as she pulled the cape over her shoulders.

"We shall see," was all she replied as she made her way from the château.

The Comtesse Laurensa was accustomed to longer flights. In fact, with her magical abilities she had learned to soar high within the heavens at greater speeds in her falcon shape. For her, a few days' journey by land was a matter of hours in her new shape. By the time she arrived at the small vale of Chambery, the paths in the village were void of people. If she had been searching for her prey unaided, she might never have found him. But with the bit of information Amadieu had given her combined with her own instincts, she searched for the financial district and began looking for the only establishment that still had a lamp burning. This did not take her long.

The only financial establishment opened had the sign of E. Thibaut Boileau hanging above the door. Through the windows she watched a single clerk who remained hunched over his desk, while the master sat close by working on his own ledgers. Using her vampire magic, Laurensa reached out to each man. She listened to their private thoughts and felt their emotions. From the clerk she felt worry and concern, his fears of making his wages to support a growing family were interspersed with thoughts of calculations, columns of numbers, and the records he kept. When she turned her attention to the master of the establishment, she received only the cold, calculating thoughts of random numbers. She could tell instantly this man cared little for humanity or the welfare of his fellow man. All he cared about was making a profit even at the expense of others. With this in mind, the Comtesse Laurensa moved toward the single door leading into the establishment.

If anyone was surprised to see the presence of a solitary woman in the finest of men's clothing, they did not show it. The clerk, an unremarkable man, glanced up at her and smiled, but before he could say anything, the Comtesse reached out with her vampire magic and waved a hand before his eyes.

"It is time for you to leave and remember nothing." Her voice was so low that one would have to strain to hear. Despite its softness, the clerk's eyes grew big with surprise, and then became glassy as he quickly closed his ledgers, returned his pen to its place, placed the cap on the ink jar, and blew out his lamp before retrieving his coat and hat from the nearby coat rack.

The Comtesse wasted little time with her prey. With something close to a growl, she turned her full attention on the man who sat nearby. His unruly shock of brown hair failed to conceal the balding on his head. His eyes, round like a fish, looked at her in surprise as his thin, delicate hands held a pen softly in his grip.

"What is the meaning..." The man's words were silenced by the Comtesse's unholy powers. With a rueful smile, she moved toward him then grabbed him by the collar. The moment she touched the mortal, she felt his entire, pathetic life pass before her. She witnessed his endeavors to secure a wife of status to bring him wealth. In disgust, she watched how he treated his children like trophies. Most importantly, she saw how he interacted within these walls.

E. Thibaut Boileau was a man of commerce, a man who valued gold above everything else. Within his own mind, he was a fair man who required no less from his workers than he gave himself. But Laurensa saw the real man. She watched as he berated those who did no bow down to him. His stinging words and accusations were trumped up charges of incompetence, yet time and again it was these very same employees who saved him from near ruin. None of this mattered to this paper-pushing autocrat. His words were final and his rule uncontested. He was a comical caricature from a Dickens novel. If he were royalty, he would have been led to the gallows along with all the other petty tyrants. However, he was not of noble blood, and this kept him safe from the laws of civil society. But her laws were neither civil nor of this society.

When she thought of all that had made her who she was, it always rankled her that she had no say whether or not she wanted eternal life. Yet sometimes she was oddly grateful to be a vampire. With her vampiric traits she had eluded the fate of many other nobles. Although there were times when she won-

dered how it might feel to lay one's head willingly upon a guil-
lotine, to never face another day of endless life, deep within her
soul she knew she had acted accordingly. It was her foresight
to keep her home and servants isolated from the social upheav-
als so that her household eluded the Reign of Terror. Of course,
if asked, she would have welcomed an end to her misery. But
even in her deepest despair she kept mindful of her servants.

Without her, who would have been there to protect them?
Who would have shielded them against the so-called people
of the Enlightenment? With a quest for scientific knowledge
and a need to uncover all mysteries, they would have hunted
vampires to dissect and study, or simply murder them for being different. The Comtesse knew she could never allow harm
to fall on her household.

Thankfully those years were all behind her. She no longer
had to worry about her home being stormed by an overzeal-
ous mob. Now that there was tranquility in the land, she used
her vampire skills to act as judge, jury, and executioner for
those who lacked humanity. Voltaire, Rousseau, and their ilk
may have rid the country of the royal elite, but they created a
whole new bourgeoisie in the merchant class. Laurensa knew
Boileau and the new wealthy class were simply pitiful excuses
for humanity. Like others before him, she would enact her punishment, and if his blood helped sate the burning deep within,
then it was all the better.

With this in mind, Laurensa released a bestial hiss and
pulled Boileau from behind his desk. At first he protested, then
grunted and tried to fight back, but her strength proved the
greater. Eventually all he could do was weep as she pulled him
from the building of commerce to the cold outdoors. Before his
protestations attracted the attention of any sentry who might
be near, she took two steps and rose into the air. The mortal,
deep in terror, wept even louder, but Laurensa did not care. She
was high above the buildings and climbing into the clouds with
her prey wiggling in her grasp. They were so high in the sky
they would look like a speck of dust to anyone on the ground,
or perhaps like a hawk with a captured rat.

"For pity sake!" The man's cries landed on deaf ears.

The few times she hunted like this she never transformed
into the falcon. Instead she kept her mortal form as she clung
to her prey. Despite his wiggling, her firm grasp on his torso did
not waver as she soared away from Chambery. With each pass-

ing moment she felt her primordial nature surface. The blood red vision submerged in her psyche bubbled to the surface. The sweet taste of victory caused her mouth to salivate, and as before, her moral compass that rose in outrage was muted against the singular need to consume her prey. When she could go no further she descended to an open field between the towns of Chambery and Grenoble. Without heed, she tossed the whimpering man to the ground before landing neatly by this side.

"Mercy! I beg of you, mercy!" The man's muffled words seeped through his tears as he lay sprawled before her, his hands risen in supplication as if this alone would bring his salvation.

"I will show you the same mercy you have shown your clerks. Remember that if you should be fortunate enough to enter the Kingdom of Heaven," Laurensa spoke in a clear, concise manner. He looked at her in shock and surprise. Before he could fully contemplate her words, she allowed the hellish nature of her curse to overflow.

With an unearthly growl, she reached down and pushed him over. In the moonlight she knew what he would see towering over him. In place of the Comtesse stood a giant, bat-like monster. As he begged for mercy she reached for him and let her animal instincts take over. With a growl and a shake, she pulled the mortal to her and bent his head aside. She brought her vampire teeth, strong enough to bite through the thick hide of a cow, to the man's neck. Careful not to kill him, she bared his neck even as he struggled in her grasp. In the red haze of her hunger she saw only the need to feed. She felt the bitter pain in the pit of her stomach as she latched upon the warm, human flesh. At the first taste of blood, her mind shouted out in triumph even as she wrestled the bigger man to the ground.

This is how the life of E. Thibaut Boileau ended. The dark forest around them grew suddenly silent even as he cried in agony. At this perfect moment in time her bloodlust could not be controlled, nor did she attempt to do so. Instead, she pinned the man down as she gorged herself to fullness. When she felt his strength wane and his muted cries vanish, she felt as if her soul rose from the darkest pits of Hell. Only when a faint glimmer of life remained did she pull herself away from the dying man.

Laurensa grunted in satisfaction as she licked the tangy liquid from her lips. Boileau's eyes, once full of life, stared up at her. In the darkness she saw the silent question that always passed before their eyes right before death consumed them. With a slight smile, the Comtesse moved to stand before the man as she looked down at him with a rueful grin. She said nothing, for nothing need be said. Instead she watched as his mortal life was extinguished for all of eternity.

So far out in the woods, only animals would find his carcass to feed upon. By the time the woodland animals finished, no one would know that this creature was once a man. With the flesh on his neck torn away and the scratches that she left upon his face, it appeared as if an animal had caught some traveler. This is exactly how she wanted this man's life to end. He would not have left a lasting legacy of admirers, therefore, it seemed only fitting he die here in the dark woods away from all of humanity. What would be left after the animals disposed of him was none of her concern. Without another thought for him, Laurensa turned her attention away from the empty husk and moved deliberately through the night.

The thirst that once banged upon her door had been abated. The madness that consumed her during the feast was slowly dissipating. Now that she was of her right mind, she could resume her normal life, if only for a short time. By the time her hunger crept on her again, she would be in control to move from flower to flower at her leisure without fear of hurting any of them. Should the unending hunger consume her again, she would find another autocrat like this man.

30 March, morning – Diary of Mademoiselle Cecilia Natashia Dupuin

I find myself suddenly queasy from tonight's session. I was able to compose myself and control my emotions, but as soon as I closed the door to my quarters I ran to the chamber pot to lose my evening meal. Although she did not say anything, I am sure the Comtesse knew of my discomfort, for she ended our session with the promise of an even more intriguing tale, a far more "bloody narration" to come, she said. I dare not ask nor contemplate what else she wishes me to hear.

Upon thinking on it, I wonder why she is so candid. She, herself, stated she is not willingly telling her tale but is doing so for the love of Madame Faivre. Why then would she be so explicit in her exploits? Surely she must know if my scribing enters into the wrong hands, it would seal her doom? But she seemed not to care. It was as if she is on a mission, or a quest of some sort, to purge her soul.

Do vampires have souls? Could they find mercy in Heaven despite acting upon their nature?

Although the Comtesse is a vampire, I sensed her remorse. No, it is true that she felt none for that ghastly man. If anything, I would have been glad to help her dispatch him to whatever fate awaited. Thanks be to God that I have never come across such a horrid person in my life. True, a few of the Sisters were harsh when I was a child, and perhaps there was a teacher here and there who did not care for us students, but for someone to openly demonstrate such a callous nature to his subordinates is something I have never encountered. Perhaps this is simply evidence of my naiveté. No, I am fortunate my first employers are kind to me. After experiencing such gentle natures I shall know from this time forward the type of people for whom I wish to work, and which to avoid.

Perhaps this is the reason for the Comtesse's candor? Day by day, with each passing transcription I feel as if I, too, am on a journey. I find myself perpetually wondering in amazement at the many things I am learning. It is hard for me to fathom just a few short months ago I was so young and living in Madame Ségolène's Finishing School for Girls. How amazing it is to realize my own personal growth simply by transcribing the lives of these two amazing women.

I am sure should anyone find my transcription they would wonder how I could call this experience amazing after hearing of the ghastly nature of a vampire. But I do. Yes, the Comtesse is a vampire, and by her own account, she was brutal. However, she was not cold. She did not take the innocence of a maiden unwillingly, nor did she kill a holy soul. No, by her words she outlined the sins of this victim, Monsieur E. Thibaut Boileau, and she dispatched him from this world in what can only be considered a quick and humane manner. If I had the power, I might not be as charitable as the Comtesse had been.

But I am being foolish. Yes, her graphic descriptions, the images she conjured sent my stomach churning and my mind reeling. I never knew such creatures truly existed. The power raging through her body and her abilities to take flight, to metamorphose, are truly amazing. I find myself wondering if there are more outside of this château who have her dark gifts?

Who would openly speak of such things? Who could be coaxed into revealing the truth that vampires do exist and live among us? Surely not the Church, and if they did admit such creatures existed, they would label them unholy abominations against God and mankind. The Church would not see the gentle, caring nature of vampires that I have seen. They would only see the threat to their own existence and would do everything in their power to eradicate them.

As I contemplate this further I find myself wondering if the tales of vampires are in fact influenced by the Church? I have no doubt they would wish us all to consider such creatures the stuff of fables. If any mortals truly believed in such creatures, then the means of their eradication would be provided. A wooden stake through the heart, the decapitation of the head, and any other sordid means for their demise are clearly established in all of the forbidden books. But are they true? How can one tell if what one reads is truth or lies?

I cause myself a great pain between my temples by this contemplation. I am a secretary, a scribe, paid to simply transcribe the words of my employers. I am not a scientist or scholar, nor a theologian who can take upon my shoulders such lofty notions. No. I shall not dwell too much upon this topic. Instead, I shall focus on my job. I shall transcribe the words of the Comtesse, and perhaps in the transcription a clearer understanding shall unfold.

30 March, evening – The recollections of Comtesse Laurensa Catherine de la Fontaine

"You seem troubled, Mademoiselle," were the Comtesse's first words. Though I feigned ignorance as I dipped my pen in the ink jar in preparation of transcribing, she must have sensed the trepidation within me, for she leaned forward from her chair and covered my trembling hand with her own.

This was the first physical contact I had with the vampire Laurensa and it is difficult to fully describe the sensations that overcame me. One would have thought that the touch of the undead was inhumanly cold, but it was not. Yes, I first felt a spark of chill run up my spine, then a cold, freezing sensation upon my skin, but it quickly vanished before a searing warmth. As if channeling the warmth of Hades, I felt her flesh like a hot coal. No sooner had I thought his than her skin grew tepid and inviting.

"I wonder, Comtesse, are there many more like you?" I found my voice weak as I dared to ask the question plaguing my thoughts.

"More of us?" The woman leaned back in her chair as her features grew kind. "You wonder if vampires have existed among you mortals all this time?"

I felt embarrassed and lowered my gaze, afraid that she would think me foolish. Instead, her voice was calm and gentle.

"Why do you contemplate these things?" Comtesse Laurensa asked me.

"I only wonder," I stammered again. "There are stories, writings that tell of vampires."

"Bah!" The Comtesse laughed heartedly as she waved away my words. "Such novels are written by amateurs or lunatic Irishmen. Do no pay them any heed. No one has ever truly gotten close enough to know the workings of my kind," she half-laughed.

"Then, the stories of how to…kill a vampire?" I ventured to say.

"Oh, they are true, mark my words. We vampires can be killed, but not with anything that is considered a 'Holy' trinket pulled out of the menagerie of tricks by the Church. Yes, we can be killed, and many have met their demise, but not with holy water, crucifixes, or a pungent herb. No, a wooden stake will do the job nicely on both vampires and mortals, but where we differ is the sun. This is the cruelest, yet most common way for a vampire to end her life," her voice softened as she looked into the burning flames of the fireplace. "I know I have thought of this time and again." Her voice was so low she probably thought I did not hear it. As if wishing to confirm, she looked at me, but I quickly lowered my eyes to my pad.

"As for are there more or us, of course, there are. I have met many, and some live as ordinary mortals. Why, you would not truly know if you saw one in a crowd at night, but I digress. I hope my words are enough to appease your curiosity, and we can move on?" She looked at me with a slight smile. The dim light in the room glimmered off her sharp, pointed teeth. I nodded courteously as I began to write her every word.

"I will now tell you of my first introduction to Madame

Faivre. It is a tale that has never been told, yet is something I believe should be known, for you see it was not a pleasant beginning. In fact, I am sure that she felt it to be quiet vile." The Comtesse turned her face away as if in shame. Her eyes remained steadfast upon the dancing flames in the fireplace as she recounted the first introduction of my employer from those many years ago...

*****

It had been many days since Laurensa's last feeding, and the land was in darkness. Winter was beginning, leading to endless days of rain. For vampires there was not much to do, nor was there anything needing to be done, except pass the time. They had been watching L'Isère River as more of a curiosity than anything. The château was far enough away that even if the river flooded over, it would not touch the estate. However, the peasants who lived nearby were greatly concerned. Nestled between Annecy and Lyon and close to Grenoble, it was a river to be reckoned with. Not only were the rising waters of concern, but also it was on nights like this that *Celle qui pleure* emerged from the darkness to take her victims to whatever hell encased her. Of course those peasants unlucky enough to be caught in the flood faced a far different fate at the hands of the vampires. Laurensa was certain that, given the choice, the mortals would rather take their chances with the *Celle qui pleure* than a mob of hungry vampires.

Before becoming a vampire Laurensa might not have believed in ghosts. Oh, she would have viewed the tales of the *Celle qui pleure* as any mortal might, with a bit of fear and then laughter at her own fright. Since becoming a vampire she knew to believe in ghosts, for she had seen them time and time again. They were simply another facet of life, an unknown entity placed upon the earth for a reason that none could fathom. Unlike vampires, ghosts were not unwelcomed in heaven. Laurensa believed they were spirits who performed some unknown yet important task. *Celle qui pleure* was no different.

Once when hunting with Amadieu, they stood at the top of the hill and watched as the majestic daemon rose from the darkness of the river. Her flowing white garments floated freely as she hovered over the waters. Then, like a hawk swooping down upon its prey, she took the men-children who stood near the river's edge. Their folly would only be known as an antecedent of the *Celle qui pleure*.

From that time forward they paid the lady her due respects. When they hunted near the river's edge, they shared their spoils with the majestic spectre. Although she had no proof, Laurensa believed the tormented spirit appreciated their common courtesy.

"There shall be no food for yet another night," Amadieu lamented.

The Comtesse Laurensa sat as she normally did, in her favorite high-backed chair before a raging fire that lighted the fireplace. The growling hunger in the pit of her stomach was easily ignored when she focused her mind upon the dancing flames. When sitting like this, watching the eternal dance of Hades, she could almost forget about the cold dampness in her château. The sounds of life and laughter were absent from the dark halls. All that remained were the handful of servants to service her every need, but lately, Laurensa had no needs or desires. Whatever she desired she kept safely harbored deep in her bosom.

As the rain pelted down upon her home, she absently listened to the words of her servant. If she closed her eyes and focused only on the wind howling through the marled halls, she could almost hear its gentle melody as it called out a single name…

But no, she would not do this. She would not torture herself. She would not allow her focus to waver.

"Listen." Amadieu arched his neck and moved close to the boarded window.

With a slight tilt of her head, the Comtesse closed her eyes and reached out with her vampiric senses. She heard the rain and wind battering against her home, then she heard the howl as it raged over the trees and moved quickly through the underbrush. Before long she heard what Amadieu heard. She sensed the presence of mortals. They were too far away to sense their thoughts, but close enough to feel their humanity. As she felt their approach she knew tonight the *Celle qui pleure* would be sated by the humans who wandered into her path.

"Come, there is enough for all." One of her servants wickedly laughed as he moved quickly to the door. As if a vote had just been cast, the rest of the vampires began to eagerly follow their comrade.

Amadieu fell in line but then stopped and looked back at her. "Are you not coming, Comtesse?" he asked with a look of concern.

"No, you go along; I have no need," Laurensa's voice came out hushed. The slender vampire stood for a moment, appearing on the verge of saying something, but then he turned to leave with only a shrug of his shoulders.

In the darkness of her home, Laurensa felt the silence of her heart. She felt no need to hunt on this night; instead, she sat in silence and lamented the loss of her beloved Isabelle. Their time together seemed short, in fact twenty years was but a droplet in the life of a vampire. She had always known her lover would perish before her, but she did not think that Isabelle would be taken so young. Even to this day, if she closed her eyes, Laurensa could hear the soft laughter echoing down the hallways. On a night like this, when the storms raged outside, they would take refuge in each other's arms, holding each other close and making sweet love. The warm, mortal body was like a silk sheet wrapped around her cold, dead heart. Whatever life Laurensa lost when she became a vampire was suddenly reignited. Like Lazarus rising from the dead, she had become alive in her lover's embrace.

Laurensa felt a strangled cry escape her control as she turned her eyes away from the flames. The tormenting memories of her lover tore a hole deep within her soul. Even though these many years had passed, her heart still ached for the touch of her mortal beauty. Her lips longed to taste the sweet softness of her Baronne.

With an animal growl Laurensa howled as she rose from her chair. The primordial beast deep within screamed out against the injustice of her existence. Filled with an unbridled rage, she grabbed the nearest table and sent it crashing against the wall. It landed with a loud boom before bursting to pieces in a shower of thin slivers, littering the marble floor. Angered at her own rage, she released a serpentine hiss and then growled before running from the room. The ever present emptiness that filled her château was a mirror of her heart, and no matter what she did, no matter how far she ran, the lonely pain of her loss bit at her heels.

In her confused and angered state, she ran through her

home and found herself climbing a familiar path. Only when she was in the pitch black darkness did she kneel upon the wooden floor of the attic and take the nearby lantern. This had been her place of refuge, her sanctuary during her long, lonely nights. Once she lit the candle within the glass, she removed the tarp from the painting and knelt before the image of her lover, Isabelle.

Tear-filled eyes gazed longingly at the oil painting. The likeness was sublime in its perfection. From the dark brown hair, the smiling rosy red lips, and captivating brown eyes, there was not a single thing that Laurensa could fault. If anyone had told her the passing of time would enhance her lover's perfection, she would have laughed or taken the opportunity to kill them. No, not time nor anything else would ever rob her of the memory of perfection that was her beloved Isabelle.

As she sat mired in her misery a sharp, sudden emotion broke through her barriers. With a tilt of her head she glanced over her shoulder into the abandoned attic. The familiar sounds of scurrying claws echoed in the room as the squeaking sounds of the rats sang a familiar tune. Ignoring their presence, she closed her eyes and reached out with her vampire senses. Her mind located a single individual crushed with emotions.

Sorrow. Pain. Despair.

Laurensa felt the melancholy thoughts of a youth trapped and imprisoned by her circumstances. In a single heartbeat she saw the future in store for this daughter of Eve and knew that life would never be the same for the female child. Before she could contemplate it, the Comtesse felt the vampires lying in wait. Amadieu, as the chief servant, would be the first to pounce upon these mortals. The others would mirror his thirst.

Laurensa shook away the sensations as she turned her gaze back to her beloved.

She did not want her sorrow muddled by what occurred in the outside world. If a young mortal wed an old man, it was none of her concern. If Amadieu took delight in his hunt, she cared even less. He and her servants had free reign over her land, and that is how she intended this night to be.

Just as these thoughts crossed her mind, her eyes rested on the sweet softness of her lover's gaze. Even in an oil painting, Isabelle's eyes called to her. The gentle wrinkles caused by her smile were never lost to Laurensa. Nor were her sparkling brown eyes that sweetly called with just a single glance. In that moment she thought she heard her beloved calling for justice from the grave. Surprised by the sound, the Comtesse jumped and looked around. She searched the rafters for the spectre of her lover, but only saw the cobwebs that swayed to and fro in the breeze.

Laurensa's brow furrowed in thought as she looked down at the oil painting. She found herself wondering if the sensation was only her imagination or the sound of her long deceased lover calling out to her. Although not prone to superstitions, she, more than anyone, knew there were greater mysteries on earth than what met the eye. Suddenly, she realized there was something calling her. It could have been Isabelle's ghost, or perhaps simply Laurensa's own conscience telling her to act, to move and protect a mortal in danger. In hope of confirming her suspicions she looked at the oil painting on last time. The familiar smile that once greeted her every day was still there, captured for all of eternity. Despite her better judgment, she made her way to the nearby window. With a single move she had the glass window open and the wooden shutters pushed back as she felt her own unearthly transformation take hold.

Rain and bitter cold jostled Laurensa, yet she kept her course. Loud thunder filled the air as bolts of lightning flashed in the distance. Ignoring it, she swooped through the air toward L'Isère River. Only when she was high above did she glide and watch the scene unfold. Her servants lay in wait as the carriage rounded the bend, but before they could overtake it, the horses reared on their hind legs, seemingly aware of the danger lurking nearby, before tearing down the road at high speed. Even through the pelting rain the shriek of a young girl was heard right before the beasts lost sight of the road and plummeted over the edge. As the carriage followed behind, the screams of horses and men alike rang through the night as they tumbled toward the swiftly moving river. Before falling into the cold river, the mass of wood and mortal flesh landed on the riverbank in a broken heap of squeaking wheels and human cries.

From her vantage point, the Comtesse noticed her servants making their way from the top of the hill. Down below, the driver of the carriage had already met his fate. A second man, hopelessly pinned beneath a wheel moaned a pitiful cry. Nearby on the muddy river bank lay the helpless form of the young woman whose fears of a doomed future reached out to Laurensa.

As she began a careful descent, the Comtesse noticed the

familiar white haze rising from the dark depth of L'Îsère River. Just as she had done before, the *Celle qui pleure* moved over the mortal bodies. Like a gentle mother, she touched the head of the dead carriage driver. A radiant haze emanated from his corpse, then flew near the gentle daemon until it was consumed. Unable to take the souls of the living, the spectre moved toward the young woman and hovered over the prone form.

"No," Laurensa hissed as she fought against the heavy winds and rain to move as close as possible to the carnage. As if hearing the vampire's plea, the mortal woman appeared to waken from the accident and just as witnessed before, the ghost made a slower retreat. Knowing that she could not take one still alive, the *Celle qui pleure* waited patiently nearby.

With a graceful move, the Comtesse landed near the river's edge and watched the scene unfold. The injured young woman attempted to move toward the man pinned below the carriage, but found her movements too painful. Laurensa was amazed such a child would attempt to help the man about to condemn her to a life of drudgery. However, she remembered the gentle spirit of her own lover, and how Isabelle often tried to help those who had wronged her. Remembering such gentleness made her melancholy.

Before Laurensa could be pulled back into sorrow, she turned her attention to the quickly developing scene before her. Her servants moved through the darkness in their varied shapes. While some liked metamorphosing into hideous shapes of abnormal beasts, others preferred the imagery conjured up by the Church. Like a mob ready to unleash its fury, the vampires scampered over the mud toward their newest victims.

Even as she moved toward the broken carriage, the Comtesse watched the scene unfold. A bolt of lightning flashed overhead and when the injured girl saw Amadieu and his cohorts, a strangled scream resembling a gasp escaped the mortal's control. Without concern for their prey, the servants scurried toward the men first, and then glanced at the horses that still lived.

"*Putain*, this one is dead!" the gardener screamed in outrage when he examined the fallen driver whose lifeless and battered body lay in a heap of flesh and blood.

Laurensa watched her servants moving through the wreckage of the broken carriage and bodies. None seemed aware of her presence as the rain and wind battered them. When the stable man moved to the mortal pinned in the wreckage, she heard his soft chuckle as he lightly touched the injured man. A high pitched scream rose from the mortal as her servants circled him menacingly. "This one lives. We can take him," the vampire said with a leering smile as he patted the top of the man's head like a child would a beloved pet.

From the corner of her eye the Comtesse watched as Amadieu set his sights on the young woman. Up until this point they had all overlooked her silent form. Laying in the mud and drenched from the rains, the young woman's fearful gaze watched their every move. Her body shook, but Laurensa did not know if it was from a chill or fear.

Amadieu approached leaning his tall form toward the fallen woman. "No, not quite," he murmured in answer to an unspoken thought.

"We can share her?" Laurensa heard the gardener ask Amadieu.

"No! Back away before I beat you!" An argument was about to ensue over who would be the first to devour the life from this mortal.

A rage, the strength of which she had never felt, welled up within the Comtesse at the thought of them killing this innocent woman. She did not know why she grew angry, nor could she have explained herself. In the past she stayed out of the hunts her servants conducted. What they did with their prey was not her concern, and she always made certain to remain neutral. Their kills were just that, theirs alone. Now, as she watched the lustful nature of her servants, an unbridled fury built. So great was her wrath that she did not hear Amadieu's response. Instead, she released an animal roar as all of her vampire powers surged forth.

Sensing her presence, her servants hissed in surprise. When a bolt of lightning flashed nearby, she took a step toward the scene. Shocked and clearly a bit afraid, Amadieu bowed low, averting his gaze. Mirroring the slender man's moves, the rest of the servants pulled back and bowed before the Comtesse's presence.

"My lady, I have a prize for you." The slender vampire tried to sooth her anger as he motioned toward the mortal woman.

It was then that Laurensa took the time to examine the woman carefully. She lay sprawled on her back, drenched from the rain and covered in mud. As if sensing a change, the young woman glanced up at her with fear and revulsion. The Comtesse noticed the cuts and scrapes, and the young woman's facial expression revealed the level of pain she suffered. Her skirt was hiked up from her plunge down the hill, yet her demureness did not diminish. Although not a doctor, Laurensa was certain that the young human was hurt far worse than she appeared.

Before her compassion took control, Laurensa gazed at Amadieu. She saw the hopeful anticipation within his eyes. In that single exchange, she had a sudden flash of insight and knew what her servant planned. He was attempting to offer this mortal to her as a way of replacing her dead lover. Once she realized this, she felt a different sort of anger rising within herself. Although she could not voice it, a part of her refused to take his offering. Nothing could ever bring Isabelle back, and as far as she was concerned, no one would ever replace the beautiful spirit which once captivated her heart.

By way of answering Amadieu, the Comtesse unleashed her anger. "I see no prize," she growled with a hiss, looking down at the mortal with disgust, "only a wet puppy." She waved her hand distractedly. "Do with her as you please."

Laurensa then turned her attention to the nearby mortal man. This was the man who was going to place the young woman into a loveless marriage. When she touched him, she saw his whole life neatly bundled in snatches of images. Filled with horror she looked down at the man as a fearful expression covered his face. *No, he would not marry her off to settle unpaid debts, for there are none,* she thought as his secret dealings were revealed to her. This was not a man with any sense of honor. Like Boileau, her victim from a week before, this man lived for profit. Today his commodity would have been living flesh. The safe delivery of the woman into the hands of a stranger would have netted him a handsome price. He did not care that the stranger was twice her age. That she was a fresh, virginal girl in the bud of womanhood only allowed him to demand a higher price for her.

When she comprehended the depth of his depravity, she yanked the man's head back and tore into his bare neck. The Comtesse was blind in her rage as she bit into the man's flesh. Unlike the gentleness she used on the maidens who offered themselves willingly, Laurensa held no regard for the man's comfort. In fact, she did all within her power to ensure his last breaths of life were as excruciating as she could make them.

Once it was over Laurensa could not help but rejoice in

her conquest. With a slight shove she pushed the near dead body over and rose to her full height. She felt the warm mortal blood dripping from her lips and down her chin, but she did not care. Instead she felt the climatic sensation, the adrenaline high that filled her after a kill. Only when she felt a sense of fear coming from the last living mortal did she pull herself from her debauchery.

When she looked down at the young woman she felt an unbridled fear like never before emanating from the girl. The Comtesse felt as if she alone was the cause of distress, and, suddenly ashamed, she ran from the broken, battered body and the scene of destruction. After she reached the top of the hill she closed her eyes in shame as the pelting rain soaked her. She stood in the darkness as her senses returned. With her hair plastered down from the rain and her clothes suddenly cold, she shook her head trying to forget the fearful gaze of the injured girl. Even as her servants moved below she remained apart from their actions.

A soft slushing sound of footfalls caught Laurensa's attention. Like a mother carrying a babe, Amadieu climbed the steep hill with his prize in his arms. Equally soaked, he held a grim expression as he moved beside the Comtesse.

"Will you take her to the village?" she asked over the din of rain.

"Of course not. She is mine," he stated firmly.

"Amadieu, you will take her to Grenoble. Let a villagers tend to her injuries," her voice grew suddenly stern as she stared at him.

"Comtesse, you told me to do with her as I will. She is mine." Amadieu's back grew stiff as he prepared to fight her over this.

The Comtesse had experienced mild insurrections before, and always she was able to smooth it over. If she had not been able to, if she had been as arrogant as the rest of the elites, she might have ended up with them upon the chopping block. Remembering this, and also realizing her servant was right, she assented, yet attempted once more to reason with him.

"What will you do with her, Amadieu, keep her as a pet?" she asked.

He tilted his head in thought, then answered with an even gaze. "I may, Comtesse. She is, after all, rather young. Perhaps she might become useful and help with cleaning the château. Or I might find other uses for her. Who knows, she might prove to be amusing," he answered. Laurensa watched after him as he carried his new charge back to the château.

As an afterthought, Laurensa shouted out through the pouring rain, lightning and thunder, "You keep your puppy out of my way! I do not ever want to see or hear her, do you understand?" In the darkness she thought she saw Amadieu nod his assent, but he was quickly swallowed by the night.

With a slight sigh, she looked back down at the carnage left behind. The rest of her servants had descended upon the living horses. Their bodies craved blood, any blood, and the horses seemed to be prime targets. As she watched them latch on to the quickly dying horses, a part of her grew disgusted. But upon reflection she realized that the beasts could not be brought up from the ravine. Most likely they were too badly injured and dying already. At least with her servants at the helm, the creatures would die quickly and be taken away by the *Celle qui pleure.*

Before she could even contemplate that thought, a hazy fog began to rise near the river's edge. Its familiar white shape grew clearer to Laurensa. Just as she had always been, the ghost wore a pristine white dress that hung past her feet. Her features were obscured by her ethereal dark hair as she looked down at the fallen prey. One by one, the daemon moved from body to body. At each one, the Comtesse saw a grey glow rise from the carcasses to join the *Celle qui pleure.*

Laurensa released an uncontrollable shudder. She was not certain which end to life was preferable; to be taken by a vampire or by this apparition. "Either fate seems worse than the other," she whispered, before turning away to make her way back to the warmth of her château.

Chapter 6

3 April, morning – Diary of Mademoiselle Cecilia Natasha Dupuin

I have had these few days to transcribe our last session, and I still find myself filled with disbelief. It is hard for me to imagine the grand dame, Madame Faivre, as the cold, frightened child on the river bank. As if the Comtesse's words were simply another fairy tale, I initially feared for the poor girl, but when I remembered that the Comtesse was describing her first meeting with Madame Faivre, I grew calm. I do not yet know how the badly broken young woman transformed into the aged matriarch. Hopefully this, too, shall be revealed.

The Comtesse has called a halt to our work for only a few days, and I cannot help but think that this is a godsend. After the last dictation I found myself leaving the session numb and silent. What was I to think after hearing such barbarity? Yet as I have had these few days to contemplate, I realize how truly valiant the noble woman is. She has shared with me her deepest shame and regrets. This condition that afflicts the nature of the vampire is one that she is yet learning to accommodate. She was placed into this predicament through no action of her own, yet she holds no regrets. She only expresses sorrow at the taking of innocent life. Even after so many years, she harbors a constant agony over her very own nature.

How strange it all seems that just a short time ago I was living in ignorant bliss in Madame Ségolène's school. The notions of vampires existed only in the forbidden fables told to titillate and amuse. I had never presumed the novels were anything more than an author's passing fancy, but I now know that these creatures of the night do indeed exist. I have learned the truth about them. Despite their foreboding nature, there is sublimeness about vampires that captivate and arouse.

I wonder if other vampires are as peaceful and kind as the Comtesse and her household. Although she has stated there are more vampires that walk amongst us, she has never said if they are benign or filled with ill will. If one were to believe the more popular novels it is hard to imagine a kind and gentle vampire. Indeed, if anything they are portrayed as fiends deserving of death. The Comtesse asked me not to believe in those writings. Although she has not read all of them, she stated that the single one she read is simply the ramblings of a madman. From this I must assume that everything I have read is false. There must be other creatures such as her who do not rejoice in killing but simply cannot help it.

Bloodlust, that is what Amadieu called it. The affliction takes over the vampire shortly after their death and rebirth into the world of darkness. The craving, no, it should be described as a need, completely consumes the vampire until they have little choice but to act upon their instincts. The properties found in blood, either of human or beast, are enough to temporarily sate their madness. I have wondered, if the blood of beasts would suffice, why not simply consume theirs rather than human blood? To this Amadieu tenderly smiled as he patted my arm as if I were an ignorant child. Like a schoolmarm at Madame Ségolène's, he gently said, "Because, my dear child, although mortals can survive on water, they cannot do so alone. Just as you need nutrient for survival, so too do we. Sadly, the nutrition we require can only be found in the blood of humans."

After hearing his explanation I do admit that there is some sense to it all. In a maddening sort of way the vampire's physiology is as miraculous as our mortal bodies. While I have not heard of any man of science or alchemy who has examined the species closely, I would venture to say vampires are of such wondrous design that like mortals, they, too, must be created by the very hand of God.

But I am not a scientist, alchemist, or theologian. I am certain if the truth were made known, the Holy Church might have some things to say on the matter. After all, are they not the ones who not only encourage but also perpetrate the injustices against any who they do not understand? Vampires would become their first target. And how sad it is, for there is much to be learned from a vampire.

I have learned so much from Amadieu. In addition to being

a valued servant of the Comtesse, he is learned. Ever since the truth of his nature was revealed, I find him easier to talk with. It is as if now that all is revealed, he is more at ease to discuss matters pertaining to humanity, and his brethren, vampires. When it comes to philosophy there seems no subject on which he is unable to educate me. I once asked him how he managed such a vast array of knowledge, and he replied, "When you have so many years on your hands, there is nothing left to do but read and study. What do you think I did during the Comtesse's dark years?"

What indeed?

I am sure that in our next session I shall learn more of the Comtesse's life and her "dark years" as Amadieu calls them. Perhaps she will explain all the mysteries regarding her initial encounter with Madame Faivre. At least I hope she does.

4 April, evening – The recollections of Comtesse Laurensa Catherine de la Fontaine

"I trust you took the time to assimilate all I have said," the Comtesse asked.

Rather than standing at the open window, the Comtesse sat in her chair facing the dancing flames within the fireplace. Her head was slightly bent, which allowed her long dark tresses to mask part of her features. Never once turning, her eyes remained fixed on the scintillating colors. As before, she wore the tailored men's breeches and white, long-sleeved shirt. Rather than having it buttoned to the top, it was opened to reveal the pale flesh below. I could not help but notice the gentle curve of her neck that swooped down to a delicate collar bone. The crest of her opened shirt revealed her cleavage partially concealed in shadows. As heat crossed my cheeks, I averted my gaze. Hesitant, I took my place by the fire, across from the large high-backed chair where the Comtesse sat.

When I remained silent, she turned to examine me. "I thought you would have been gone by now," she stated nonchalantly.

"Why would I leave?" I asked, a bit surprised by her words.

"My words, my narration must surely have repulsed you."

"My Lady, Comtesse, I am here to dictate your words, not to cast judgment," I replied in a steady voice.

She stared at me. Her grey eyes seemed ablaze with emotions as she examined me closely. For what felt like years, her eyes held mine. As if I were passing inspection, the Comtesse nodded slightly as she returned her attention to the fireplace.

"By now you wish to know the rest of the story? You wish to know what became of Ni...Madame Faivre?" she asked in a gentle voice.

"Yes, Comtesse, if it is your wish," I replied glancing down at my pen and pad, preparing to commence my dictation.

"My wish," her voice was filled with such sorrow that I looked up from my pad. She appeared not to notice me as she continued to gaze at the warming flames.

"Madame?" I spoke softly as the wood crackled with life. When she did not answer, I leaned toward her and lightly touched her long sleeve shirt. As if surprised by the contact, Comtesse Laurensa looked at me sharply. Her eyes narrowed upon me for a scant moment, then averted quickly.

"Vampires are not supposed to have wishes; we are expected to have all that we desire. Isn't that how they write us?" she turned her question upon me.

I thought over her words. I could sense the extreme pain and sadness but did not know why. It appeared that an answer was needed, yet I could not find my voice.

Sensing my distress, she released a soft chuckle as she leaned back within the comfort of her chair. "Child, you are easy to read," she smiled broadly, which revealed her two sharp canine teeth.

"C-C-Comtesse?" I found myself stuttering.

She smiled at me for only a moment before averting her gaze. "Come and let us begin our tasks, you and I," she said with a sound of resolve in her voice.

"Initially it was not hard to ignore Amadieu's new pet. Yes, mark my word, she was his pet. He was always prone to bringing home strays, a weak and feeble girl here, a child there, always the same. They were lost or in need of assistance, and he, ever charitable Amadieu, would take them in and nurse them back to health as if they were birds that had fallen from a nest. But none ever survived long. Sometimes they simply succumbed to their injuries or illness. Sometimes they wandered away and were taken over by the creatures that existed outside of my château," she explained as her gaze grew distant with memories.

"It was not hard having the mortal girl here at first, because she was never felt, never seen. It was as if it had never happened, and if it did not, then I could go along in my endless days as I have always done." The Comtesse frowned as she remembered those days from long ago...

*****

Night after endless night Laurensa marked the days in lonely silence. Without Amadieu, it felt like she had no one to talk to. Yes, there was Constance, the stableman, and François, the gardener who no longer tended to the gardening. There was even Étienne, the house-boy who once assisted with the general maintenance of the château. There were other servant vampires roaming through her household, but she did not have the same relationship with them as she had with Amadieu. She did not know if it was because he was the only original vampire in the staff who remained loyal to her, or because he was the highest ranking staff member.

When Laurensa first arrived at the château, Amadieu was her husband's valet. He was responsible for tending to her husband's every whim. From bathing him, to dressing, and to providing willing sexual partners, it fell to Amadieu to do everything for his master. In theory the valet was even expected to protect his master, but this was not the case for Amadieu. Not only did he not protect Laurensa's husband, but there were rumors that he had aided in the vampire's demise.

As a wife it would have been her duty to seek revenge upon the household staff responsible for her husband's untimely death, but having only been married a short time, and existing an even shorter time as a vampire, Laurensa held no loyalty to the man. In fact, like the servants, she rejoiced in his death. Soon afterward, Amadieu's duties shifted and he began to act as her personal assistant. If any had thought this odd, no one ever mentioned it. Instead they accepted the new shift in power, and with Amadieu's help, Laurensa was able to carry the family forward. It was for this reason that she grew attached to the enigmatic vampire.

If she was anything like her husband, she would not have allowed Amadieu to bring home a pet. In fact, she would have dispatched it quickly. But she was not her husband. Yes, she would rather Amadieu take the young woman to Grenoble where a villager could tend to the injured mortal, but her word was solid, even if spoken in haste. She had given him this puppy, and he had promised to keep the young girl out of sight. This was why she found herself suddenly alone.

In the beginning she saw little of her friend. He was always by the mortal's side doing all that he could to keep her alive. Not a healer by nature, he had learned the physiology of mortals over the years and knew the rudiments of healing. If Laurensa had not been walled up within her grief, she might have looked outside of her own situation and had pity on the girl. But she did not. In fact, the longer that the girl was in the château, the more the Comtesse missed her long dead lover.

Every day before the sun rose, Laurensa made her way to the safety of the mausoleum located under the château. Unlike the graveyard behind the home, the mausoleum was a place outsiders seldom visited. The entrance was located at the back of the large marble kitchen; its door nestled inconspicuously out of the way. Only those who grew up here knew of its location and how to make their way through the labyrinth of underground catacombs. As soon as Laurensa was initiated into the darkness, she soon learned the way to her own place of protection.

Although all of the château windows were barred from the sun, every break of day found the vampires making their way down into the icy cold depths. The candles that lit the way were never necessary because they could see better in the darkness than in daylight. Despite this, Laurensa insisted the candles be lit as a demonstration of the shred of humanity which remained in them. As she made her way down the winding staircase and through the deep, cold tunnels, she gave cursory nods to her vampire servants. Deep in this pit was a room of opulent design. Within it sat a single coffin. Once, when her husband was still a vampire, there were two coffins side by side. But now a widow, there remained only one.

When Laurensa entered the chamber she placed her candle in the holder and moved to the dark box. In her customary manner she removed her outer coat and left it nearby as she lifted the lid and lay within it. Once lowered, she was able to close her eyes to rest. The sounds of vermin that scuttled nearby were like gently chirping birds to her senses. Their long, slender tails dragging through the dirt sounded like butterfly wings. As the sun rose in the sky, she spent her days like this, eyes closed to the world as she dreamt vampire dreams.

Many times she dreamt of her lover, Isabelle. She missed her dearly and mourned for the days from long ago. When Isabelle lived, the Comtesse did not sleep in this coffin. Instead she lay in the arms of her lover. Their room was the master suite and within it they had all they desired. Sometimes Isabelle would rise quietly and leave Laurensa to rest while she moved about the château by day. Yet there were other times when the mortal would forgo her duties to cling to her vampire lover. On days like this, they spent the time in periodic lovemaking and sleeping. The cares and concerns of the outside world did not penetrate into their sanctuary, and this is how Laurensa preferred it to be.

Now that her lover was gone, the Comtesse could do little but retreat to the safety of her coffin. If her servants thought this strange, none mentioned it. They simply took it as a matter of course that her habits would change until it became routine. While she slept in the day, she dreamt of the days when Isabelle was alive. But somewhere along the line her mind began to wander. The vampire gifts at her command reached out like silky tendrils to the mortal healing just a few floors above her. When she first tapped into the young woman's dreams Laurensa thought this was just another dream of mortal existence. But when she dreamt of the accident over and over again, she knew that she had inadvertently entered into the memories of Amadieu's pet, and it angered her. Laurensa was angry at her own lack of control and angry that the blissful feelings of life could consume her so. More importantly, she was angry at the memories the girl's presence elicited.

With each passing day the girl lived, Laurensa was reminded of Isabelle's death. The life that slowly returned to this puppy of a child had affected Laurensa deeply. Without Amadieu to talk to, she found herself going every night to the attic where the painting of her lover sat.

There was a time when the grand painting hung in the main foyer for all visitors to see. The beauty of the mistress of the château was not something that Laurensa tried to hide. In fact, she was proud of the Baronne and even prouder she had chosen Laurensa as a lover and mate. After the plague swept through the land and many mortals died, including Isabelle,

Laurensa could not stand to be reminded of what she had lost. She removed it and carefully took it to the attic where it was lovingly covered with a tarp for protection.

Now, after so many days with Amadieu's puppy nearby, Laurensa spent her long, lonely nights near the only image that gave her comfort. Sometimes in her grief she wept until her energy was spent. Once or twice she woke when Amadieu gently picked her up and carried her down to her coffin, but he never stayed long. He simply patted her on the shoulder and closed the lid in order to return to nursing his injured pet. If Laurensa had any resentment over this, she did not voice it. Instead she tried her best to hold on to whatever sanity remained buried within her grief.

One particular night when she sat before the painting, she heard her friend speaking softly behind her but did not clearly hear his words. When he tapped her on the shoulder, she turned and looked up at him. He wore a long coat and a hat. In his hands Amadieu held his black leather gloves.

"Comtesse, my apologies, but I must leave for a short time," he stated as he knelt before her.

"Leave?" Laurensa was confused as she looked into her friend's eyes. Her brows furrowed and a frown crossed her features.

"Yes, Comtesse. I have need to travel, but I will not be gone long. I shall be back in a few weeks," he explained gently. "I have left instructions with the servants. As for Nina, she will not venture from the room. I promise. She has ample supplies and water. I will be back by the time it runs out."

"Nina?" Laurensa looked down at the dark wood floors of the attic as she tried to remember the name.

"The girl, Comtesse. Her name is Nina. Agnes Brigitte Faivre, but she prefers to be called Nina. I have already spoken to her, and she shall not cause you any trouble. I promise, until I return you will not even know that I was gone." He smiled gently as he lightly ran his slender fingers through Laurensa's hair, pushing the strands back behind her ears.

"Isabelle..." She looked back at the picture, but could not finish her sentence.

"I know, love, I know. She is gone and you are ill. I know this," he said as he knelt by her side, pulling her close to gently rock her in his arms. "Someday, Comtesse, it will not hurt so much. Someday..." He did not finish his sentence instead he pulled back, turned her face to him. With a beautiful smile he wiped Laurensa's tears from her cheeks and then held her face in the palms of his hands.

"I shall be back soon, Comtesse. Do not fret," he promised before placing a tender kiss upon her forehead.

Laurensa did not know how many days had passed since Amadieu left. Whatever pain a vampire could feel now filled her entire being. Each night she found herself climbing the familiar stairs to sit in front of the painting of her lover. The grief and sorrow poured from her until she did not know what else to do but allow it to spill forth.

One night she heard a slight creaking on the stairway entrance. Her head tilted sharply as her ears focused in on the sound. Laurensa felt her nostrils flaring as she picked up the familiar scent of a mortal. She could smell the young woman's sweat; the tangy aroma wafted through the room. At first the Comtesse felt the intoxication of the mortal's presence. Her animal nature rose from deep within her until all she could see was the blood red life flowing within the young woman's veins. The primordial beast that resided in all vampires took control of her senses. With supernatural abilities, she jumped from her place and towered above her natural height. Through blood red eyes she glared down at the mortal and bared her fanged teeth while releasing an inhuman hiss.

Nina's high-pitched scream echoed through the rafters right before she dropped her candle and turned to flee. Angered by the intrusion into her private domain, the Comtesse chased after the girl. She fluttered her wings and flew down the staircase. Once or twice, she reached out to snag the girl's nightshirt, but missed her mark. With a growl-like howl, she chased her through the corridors and down a flight of steps. Only when she came within a hair of grabbing the intruder, the girl made her way into the safety of her room.

The bone jarring slam of the door left Laurensa breathless. From inside the room the mortal bolted the door and locked it tight. Shocked, the Comtesse opened her eyes as she felt herself panting out of control. Had she wanted to, she could have barreled the door down and taken the mortal, but she did not. This room was a sanctuary set up by Amadieu, and she would not defile it. Instead, she stood outside the door in silence. Her body slowly morphed back to normal, and she found herself leaning against the wooden door, her palms laid flat against the surface.

From inside she heard the frantic thoughts of the girl as she continued screaming in fear. A part of Laurensa reached out hoping to touch the mortal spirit. When she did, she felt a soothing contact almost familiar in nature. Despite the fear, this young woman's soul was as Amadieu described. She was gentle and kind.

With a stifled cry the Comtesse broke contact and fell to the floor outside the door. Her fingers lightly rested on the door as if begging for help. As silent tears fell unheeded down her cheeks, Laurensa leaned her head against the cold wood and closed her eyes. Despite the pain and agony of her sorrow no one came to her assistance.

Inside the room, she heard the mortal moving around, attempting to find a place of refuge. The sound of metal and fabric rose as the curtains were drawn around the bed, and then the room grew silent. When Laurensa reached out toward the mortal's soul, the only thing she could feel was the young woman's fear and repulsion of the unholy spectre she had just seen. When Laurensa felt it, she rose silently from the floor and moved away slowly on shaky legs. After a few steps, she looked back at the barred door. A part of her wished she could knock on the door, call out that there was no need to fear, but she did not.

"Too soon," she heard herself whisper as she turned and walked away.

When she was safe within her private parlor, Laurensa sat in her favorite chair. She closed her eyes, allowing her mind to wander in a dream-like trance. As the darkness of the night surrounded the château, she reached out with her mind. Like a succubus of lore, she allowed her magical vampire abilities to reach out to the only mortal close by. As the girl slept, Laurensa's mind merged with hers, and for this night she took the mortal to heights never before experienced. Although fearful, Nina lowered her guard and allowed the Comtesse's first immortal touch upon her soul.

From that night forward Laurensa knew that she would be allowed her privacy to grieve. Although she did grieve nightly for the loss of Isabelle, she also found herself traveling through her mind to the young woman who remained hidden behind a locked door. No one could have explained to the grieving Comtesse that her longings and needs were normal, because she was beyond reason. All she knew was she struggled each and every night to banish the pain and fought against the urge to greet the morning sun for one last time.

5 April, morning – Diary of Mademoiselle Cecilia Natashia Dupuin

How sad and lonely the Comtesse was. I find myself reading over my transcription. I can see why Madame Faivre insisted I hear her mate's story, for indeed, this is what they are. I am not certain how they came to be so close, but I am privileged to be allowed to hear of the beginning of their relationship. The trust that is bestowed upon me warms my heart.

I am saddened to hear of the Comtesse's lonely existence. To think that she would even contemplate ending it just tears my soul. She was so grieved by the loss of her lover, the Baronne, that she could not even see the possibilities existing before her. Thankfully she seems to have understood, for today they are as close as any lovers could be.

I wonder if I shall ever find such love. I had lamented the same thing when hearing of the romance between the Comtesse and Baronne, and now that I see the closeness of Madame Faivre and the Comtesse, I find myself wondering this again. Is it possible that there is such a great love for more than one mortal woman?

I blush to think of this, for I have never thought this way before. Yes, I experienced many things with Margarie and even longed to be together forever. But alas, it was not meant to be, for she fell in love with a man. Who am I to think that my unnatural proclivities could someday find happiness? How many others like me exist, I wonder?

Yet the Comtesse and Madame Faivre had no trouble finding each other. Of course this could all be attributed to the Comtesse's vampire abilities. How often does such a circumstance exist? No, although a romantic and foolish notion, I do not believe I am destined for such happiness. But still, is it wrong to hope?

5 April, evening – The recollections of Comtesse Laurensa Catherine de la Fontaine

"Do you think me a fiend for what I did?" the Comtesse asked me.

I sat down in my chair with my pad in hand and looked at the dark figure sitting in the shadows. To make her point more clear, she leaned forward into the diffused light. Her eyes were glowing red and her teeth far more pronounced than I ever recalled.

"Am I evil in your eyes for entering into the dreams of Madame Faivre?" she asked again.

"No, Comtesse, I do not see you as evil."

She examined me closely before releasing a sigh. She closed her eyes and leaned back into the shadows as her hands rested loosely upon the armchair. With only the crackling of the burning fire, we sat in silence. When she began to speak, her voice was low and calm. "I repulsed myself. I never wanted to, never thought I would but..." Her voice trailed off as she leaned her weary head upon a bent arm.

"You were ill, Comtesse. You were grieving and not of your right mind. Surely you were in a weakened state?" I offered humbly.

She looked up at me in silence and nodded as she closed her eyes again.

"Amadieu was, of course, correct. I knew what Nina, that is, Madame Faivre was doing," the Comtesse said. "Whenever she left the château I felt her spirit soaring. I felt her filled with such life that it took my breath away. Yes, she literally took my breath away."

The Comtesse rose from her place and paced the length of the room. With her head bent and shoulders slumped, she seemed deep in thought. I could not help but notice her womanly shape concealed beneath the men's clothing. Perhaps when she wore a jacket or overcoat, her shapely hips were concealed, but now, wearing only the trousers and white shirt, there was no mistaking her gender. Even if one did, she would surely notice her long locks or hair falling in gentle waves past her shoulders. As I examined the Comtesse I noticed that there was a mixture of power and vulnerability within her. I was in awe of the power she controlled, yet I was filled with sorrow for her. I wanted to hold her in my arms and protect her against the harshness that life brought to her. When she turned, her eyes remained level.

"There was a part of me that wanted to kill Madame Faivre. You know that, don't you?" she asked with a whisper, a tinge of shame etching her words.

"Yes, Comtesse," I answered as I waited for her to begin the transcription for the night.

"I think my servants were ready to kill her if it hadn't been for Amadieu. No, Mademoiselle, I could not kill her." She waved away my surprise. "Not after I touched the purity of her mind. Once you have touched such a sublime gift of God, you cannot ever wish to harm it. That is what her gentle spirit was to me," she said as she moved back to sit in her chair. "Her sheer terror brought forth her humanity," the Comtesse half whispered.

"Perhaps in letting her read the letters between Isabelle... the Baronne, and I, I was calling out to her for help? Perhaps I wanted her to read them so that she would understand the hideousness that I am?" The Comtesse's words trailed off.

"You are not hideous, Comtesse," I tried to assure.

She looked directly at me. Her eyes grew stern and then, before I realized a change, she hastily stood up. Like a demon of the night, she shifted and transformed before my eyes until she was the large beast described in my past transcriptions. I could not help but release a slight yelp as I dropped my pen. Moving further back into my seat, I gazed up into the face of the creature of the night. Its slender oblong head was covered with a mass of grey hair, its eyes, yellow and beady, sat on the sides of its head. A short snout formed its nose, and its mouth opened to reveal long razor-sharp teeth. Arms that once rested lightly at the Comtesse's side were thin and covered in fine filaments of hair. Attached to the arms was a thin membrane that unfurled like the wings of a bat. Her slender fingers were transformed into sharp, menacing talons.

When I collected myself, I blinked in surprise, then released a sigh as I leaned over to retrieve my pen from the floor. "I must say, that is impressive," I commented as I straightened myself in preparation of the dictation.

The Comtesse's shape changed back to that of the beautiful woman who I have come to know. With a hearty laugh, she sat down upon the chair as the air in the room became welcoming once more. She seemed at ease, and, in response, I relaxed. Slightly smiling, she leaned forward, her hands clasped in her lap.

"So, I did not frighten you?" she asked.

"Perhaps startled is a more appropriate word," I suggested.

"Yes, startled. That is good. I startled Madame Faivre as well. There was nothing that I could have said to wipe the image of the hideous beast that attacked her from her mind. I had to find a way to reach her. Yes, Amadieu was correct. She would not have found my correspondence had I not allowed her to," the Comtesse stated. Then, with a slight sigh, she leaned back in her chair. "Perhaps it was simply the right place and time. Perhaps it was necessity. I could not have seen it then, I might not have accepted it, but Amadieu was correct. Madame Faivre is what was needed, and if I had to allow her to read my most private words that were shared with a lover, then so be it. At least then she would not always see me as a monster."

With this, the Comtesse settled farther into her chair. She paused for only a moment. Staring into the bright flames of the fire, she seemed to be collecting her thoughts or organizing her mind. When she was ready, she turned and continued to tell the tale...

****

Logically, Laurensa knew that only a week had passed since Amadieu left, but for her it felt like an eternity. Night after endless night she found herself entering the mind of the young woman. On the nights when the mortal did not dream, Laurensa made her way to the attic to gaze upon the loveliness of the painting. Sometimes when she was in her deepest grief she thought she heard the voice of Isabelle cooing sweet words of love and encouragement. More often, she was faced with the sounds in the attic. The rafters creaked from the coldness outside. A click, clank sound of mice scurrying to and fro cut through the darkness. Occasionally she caught one of the furry beasts that ventured too close to her place of mourning and drank of its blood to quench her thirst. Alone in such a place she was at ease to grieve to her heart's content.

The Comtesse had not admitted it to herself, but her loneliness and sorrow had grown stronger since the arrival of their injured guest. After their initial encounter and her subsequent entering into the girl's dreams, Laurensa had touched a spirit remarkably similar to Isabelle's. The ability to sense the gentle nature, to revel in the folly of youth took hold of the vampire until all she could think of was her lost lover. Night after endless night she wept before the canvas. In the day as she lay in her coffin she felt the joyful explorations of the mortal and smiled as vampire tears escaped her closed eyes.

On a night she would never forget, the Comtesse sat mourning before her lover's image. She was so deep in grief that the sounds of soft footfalls never caught her attention. Instead, she remained sitting completely oblivious to the young woman who stood frozen nearby.

"Oh, my dear sweet one," Laurensa whispered softly, her eyes scanning every line of her lover's face. "Too long, my love, too long. We had so little time together, and now I am truly alone." She wept uncontrollable. Not even the presence of the mortal caused her to turn away from her grief. "Oh my Isabelle, my very own love. How we were so happy, so content," she whispered.

It was then that Laurensa felt the presence of an intruder. With head bent, she felt the burning warmth of the mortal close by. Her nostrils flared as she inhaled the scent of the young woman. All around her, she suddenly heard the loud beating of this woman's mortal heart. Angered by the intrusion and enraged by the audacity of the guest to intrude upon her most private moments, Laurensa felt the full force of her vampire nature rising deep within.

"You!" The Comtesse rose in a flash and towered over the weak and frail mortal. Her body had morphed into the same hideous creature that had chased the girl down the hall. "Leave me be!" Laurensa screeched as she unfurled her arms and allowed the bat-like wings to mask the single lantern in the room.

"I-I…" Nina tried valiantly to speak, but stood frozen in fear. After what seemed an endless amount of time, she let out a blood curdling scream, dropped her candle, and turned to flee. Laurensa watched the whole thing as if she were outside her body. When the candle dropped, she felt an animal howl escape her control as she tore off after the young woman.

How dare she interrupt my mourning! The Comtesse's mind raced as the anger began to boil. *How dare she look at me in disgust! She is a guest who was told to mind her own business, yet she interrupts me time and again!* Laurensa silently cursed as she chased the mortal through the château.

Nothing would get in her way. Neither an eternity of ever-lasting life nor the recrimination of a young pup would sway her anger. The look of terror from the girl spoke mountains to Laurensa as she pursued the girl through the château. Once or twice, she lunged in an attempt to grab the mortal, but only managed to snag the cloth of her dress. As the terror-filled screams echoed through the corridors, Laurensa gave chase. She felt the bestial impulses well up and pure adrenaline coursed through her being. When she saw the girl running into the cemetery a wicked grin crossed her lips as she realized that she would finally, once and for all, be rid of the nuisance in her home. Just as the Comtesse was ready to catch her, she stopped in her tracks and watched as the girl twirled in a circle. Her frightened eyes darted all around and for the first time, Laurensa felt the full weight of fear pouring from the girl's spirit.

When Laurensa looked up at the angle of mourning, she was taken aback by the tears that fell unheeded. The statue's fathomless eyes stared directly at her. The marble guardians put into place to protect her beloved Isabelle now looked down at her with recrimination. Their heads tilted slightly as their anguished expressions focused on her. Although they did not speak, Laurensa felt their admonishment clearly. As if Isabelle were their guiding conscience, the supernatural effigies cast forth their disapproval. With a deep sigh, the Comtesse lowered her head in shame.

In the short time she had been with Isabelle, she never caused her fright. She never purposely unmasked her full evil to torment the gentle woman. Yet now she did so to this girl, wantonly and with disregard. Although Isabelle was no longer living, Laurensa felt as if her lover's spirit was casting down her judgment through the holy statues. The utter sense of loss that once filled Laurensa's soul was now replaced with shame, and all she could do was lower her head.

She was so caught up in her shame she did not hear her servant nearby. As if masked by his vampire gifts, he appeared before them dressed as before. His long overcoat hung loosely and his face was hidden in shadows. Like a lioness protecting its cub, he moved to the young mortal. When Laurensa heard the mortal's voice, her self pity and sorrow was replaced with shame.

"Oh, Amadieu!" the girl wept as she wrapped her arms around his neck. Amadieu held her close and cooed softly as he glanced at the Comtesse, a look of apology mixed with sadness crossing his eyes before he turned his attention back to the girl. Laurensa turned away slightly as she fought to catch her bearing, to pull herself together lest this mortal see her true vulnerabilities. As they spoke softly, the Comtesse's brow turned into a frown.

"Amadieu, what have I said of your little pet?" Laurensa's voice was stern in a play to hide her weakness. She allowed her anger to seep through every word. Amadieu pulled his charge behind him and stood between them.

Although they were friends, he was still a servant and knew how to properly address her. With head bowed, he kneeled before her and lowered himself in supplication. "My Lady, forgive me. The child is young; I should not have left her unattended for so long," he offered as he tugged at the girl until she was pulled down beside him.

The Comtesse never allowed her eyes to waver. She stared down at the young woman. Laurensa's bearing, no longer in the shape of a monster, remained steadfast. She did not waver as she glared at Amadieu's pet. In the silence of the early morning, she watched and waited for the girl to speak. Just when it seemed that the mortal's lips would bring forth words, the girl's eyes rolled back into her head as her body fell forward. With little grace, the young woman fell face first into the muddy soil.

Laurensa shook her head as she released a tired sigh. "Well, do you not think you had better take her in before she catches her death of cold?"

Equally surprised, Amadieu glanced down at his charge, then rose quickly and whisked her up in his arms. "Of course," he said as he began to carry her into the château.

The Comtesse remained standing outside in the dark. She heard the distant sound from the forest. The creatures that thrived by night were out in full force, but she knew that her château was safe. When she glanced up at the marble statues, they were all in their normal positions. The mourning angel remained splayed over her marble tier, her face now hidden from view. The circle of statues looked upon the mausoleum as they kept a watchful gaze upon the crypt. Within the intricately detailed walls rested the casket of Isabelle, her first and only lover.

Laurensa released a tired sigh as she turned away from the sad memories of the woman who had captivated her undead heart. She did not know why Amadieu's pet had spurred such emotions within her. She could not explain why, for a split second, she wanted to kill the girl. All she knew was her heart was aching. With this melancholy thought, she returned to the warmth of her château.

6 April, mid-afternoon – Diary of Mademoiselle Cecilia Natashia Dupuin

I never thought such things could be real, yet I know that vampires do exist. Why then is it so strange to think of statues, inanimate objects, as becoming alive? I remember seeing them during my many walks through the grounds. The description of the cemetery by both Madame Faivre and the Comtesse is vastly different from the way I found it. It does not have an abandoned feel. The grounds, even in winter, hold a neat and organized appearance. Now that spring I upon us I can see the gardener's skillful care of the shrubs and flowers. By the time spring is in full force there will be such a beautiful array of floral scents. The colors of the flowers will light up any despondent soul, and the sounds of nature shall rise into the air. No, the cemetery is vastly different than the early days when Madame Faivre first arrived, and perhaps she is the cause of this?

There are some days when, after a session with the Comtesse, I see the head grounds keeper entering into the matriarch's room. I do not know how long he stays, but I'm certain he remains long enough for Madame Faivre to pass along her wishes and desires for her garden. How interesting it is that she has incorporated such beauties of nature on such hallowed ground. As I contemplate it I can see the soundness of her thinking. The peaceful place where the bodies of past generations rest is indeed worthy of such beauty. When sitting among the tombs and flowers I feel the harmonic balance of life and death. Yes, I am certain that the beautiful landscape can be credited to Madame Faivre.

There has been some movement of late. I notice that the physician of Grenoble was called. He arrived at day break with the day servant, went directly to Madame Faivre's room, and stayed for a few hours. I must have fallen asleep because, when I awoke, he had gone. Amadieu said he left as quietly as he arrived. The tall vampire was amused by the healer's actions for it seems that, although he will come out when regularly called, he will only do so by daylight and will never consent to spend the night.

"It is as if he thinks that we would actually consider his blood worthy of taking," Amadieu said with a soft chuckle and a bit of a twinkle in his eyes.

It appears that aside from their mortal servants, who resided within the château for a few decades, I am the first to have stayed for so long as a guest. Amadieu said this bodes well, but for what, I do not know. I asked him what he meant, but he donned an innocent expression and said that he spoke out of turn, and I was not to contemplate it any further.

This place is so queer. Just when I begin to think that one mystery is revealed another becomes evident. I do not fully understand what Amadieu is keeping from me. Perhaps by the time my position is finished and the transcription is turned over to Madame Faivre, there will no longer be any mysteries surrounding the château or its occupants.

6 April, evening – The recollections of Comtesse Laurensa Catherine de la Fontaine

"Mademoiselle, I am certain by now that you understand Madame Faivre and I did not start out...on friendly terms?" the Comtesse asked as she moved to take her place in the high-backed chair. I sat in my customary place as I readied my pad and pen.

"Yes, Comtesse," I said.

She released a tired sigh as if recalling those days drained her of energy. She leaned her head back and closed her eyes while I sat quietly next to her. In the distance I heard the echo of the large grandfather clock in the hallway ringing ten. If there were any servants nearby, the silence masked their presence. Just when I thought the Comtesse had fallen asleep, her low, tired voice began.

"Things were difficult for me at the time. Amadieu will say that I was ill, but can a vampire who is immune to both sickness and death be ill?" She asked rhetorically. She sat slumped in her chair, her legs crossed and stretched out before her and her arms resting comfortably on the chair. If she watched the flames in the fireplace, I do not know because her gaze grew distant. I noticed, for the first time, a fatigue within her posture. It seemed the burden of life weighed heavily upon her shoulders, while the Comtesse paused in bleak silence.

"Perhaps he was right. Perhaps I was ill, but not in the conventional way. You see, Mademoiselle, I was ill of heart. Never in my mortal life did I think I would ever find someone to complete me. Always I grew up with the notion that romantic love was not meant for me, that I would be wedded to a man whose social position and stature would enhance my father. And so it happened that I entered into a loveless marriage. But upon my husband's demise, I found myself suddenly free to rule my own life, to find love to fill my heart, and I did. Isabelle was the one, but, alas, our time together seemed far too short," the Comtesse lamented.

"I spent many lonely years after her death. Time passed by as it always does for a vampire, and with each passing day I found myself slipping deeper and deeper into a chasm of darkness. I could not see beauty around me, I could not feel or experience it. It was as if a veil had been placed before my eyes... until Nina," the Comtesse's voice grew thoughtful. "Nina, that is Madame Faivre, was able to bring light back into my existence. But it was no easy feat for her." The Comtesse chuckled.

I found myself smiling up at the Comtesse when I heard the unfamiliar sound, for I was barely becoming accustomed to her merriment. She did not notice my smile as she continued her narration. In turn I quickly wet my pen, ready to begin our nightly dictation.

"I would never admit to Amadieu that he was right, that I was losing myself to the loneliness and despair. That I was ill and in need of healing, and that Nina was the cure, no." She shook her head in dismay. "My own pride and arrogance prevented me from admitting that he was right, but he was. I was losing myself, and Nina found me," she said as her gaze grew thoughtful. She leaned back in her chair and released a sigh. It was not one of relief, nor one of dread. It simply was a sound that allowed her to regroup her thoughts. Perhaps it was even her way of giving herself permission to tell the tale from long ago...

*****

Laurensa knew that the mortal wanted to whisk Amadieu away. As she lay in her coffin she could clearly hear their conversations. She knew the young woman's fears and could feel her disgust, but Laurensa was helpless to do anything. There was a part of her that wanted to go to the woman and talk to her, to tell her of her sorrows and beg her forgiveness, but she couldn't bring herself to do so. Instead, she did her best to keep away from the second floor of the château. After all, the mortal was Amadieu's pet, and as such, it was his duty to interact with her. Besides, Laurensa felt at a loss for words.

She had frightened the girl. For some unknown reason, this mortal struck a chord in her, and it caused pure rage to spill forth. Yes, this had happened many times while hunting, but never in her home. Certainly not with a defenseless woman. Her parlor games and mystical gifts she reserved for those who deserved to feel true horror before their deaths. Not even Isabelle had ever experienced her true nature, and this shamed Laurensa. If Isabelle were alive today, she would surely have scolded her. It did not matter if Laurensa was of higher social rank, Isabelle would never allow an injustice to go unpunished. The very idea that her lover would be disappointed with her was enough to weigh upon Laurensa's heart.

Thankfully the mortal failed to convince Amadieu to leave. If she had, Laurensa was not sure what she would do. How could she get along without her trusted friend? No, she could not. With the loss of Isabelle she was near the end of her strength. All it would take was one more blow before she would voluntarily take the final walk into the rising sun. Who could blame her? Having lived so many years only to lose the one soul who made you whole was something most mortals could not bear. Why then should she be different?

Once that fateful day was over, life at the château returned to normal. Amadieu and the girl spent a great deal of time together. After that day Laurensa did not bother to listen to their prattle and instead found herself, once again, locked within her grief. The only thing that changed was that Amadieu made certain to spend more evenings with the Comtesse, even if it was only to sit before the fire's flames in silence.

On a day when Amadieu excused himself early, the Comtesse found herself alone in her study. Her mind always returned to the happy times when Isabelle was in her arms. Sometimes if she listened hard enough, she could hear the gentle laughter of her deceased lover echoing through the halls. Filled with sorrow, Laurensa left her study and made her way to the attic just as she had done so many times before. When she knelt before the painting, she lit the nearby lantern, then pulled the tarp away and gazed at the exact replica of the only soul she had ever loved. She did not know how long she sat there; she only knew that the grief within came welling up like molten lava until she wailed in sorrow and despair. Vampire tears that cried for no one else flowed freely down her cheeks. Only when she heard the floor boards creaking behind her did she pull herself from her lamentations. With a slight sniff of the air, she smelled the mortal nearby. Angered by the intrusion Laurensa growled deep within her chest as she darted up and turned upon the young woman.

"I told you!" Laurensa's vampire magic transformed her into the beast again as she towered over the smaller woman. Lifting her arms, her wings spread to their full span, and, for a moment, she felt glee at the clicking of her long fingernails. Before her, the young mortal seemed on the verge of tears or fleeing, but she did not move. Instead, she remained steadfast as she stood before the Comtesse. Through the haze of her anger, Laurensa saw the woman's tears falling and wondered what had caused her sadness. When the mortal shook her head and remained in her place, Laurensa was in disbelief.

"No. I will not obey." The mortal remained firmly planted in place. She tilted her chin up, daring Laurensa into action.

Laurensa stood before her in silence. She felt confused, or perhaps moved, but the strength and conviction in the girl's words. When it appeared as if time had stood still, she allowed herself to morph until her body was once again human. Despite the change, she towered over the house guest. By the diffused light of the lantern, she searched for the young woman's sincerity. Although she longed for it to be true, she did not want to believe such a pure and young heart could ever find forgiveness for all her trespasses. But as she examined the dark eyes, Laurensa released the breath she had been holding as she realized there was only forgiveness and...something else that she could not fathom. When she finally understood what it was, the Comtesse fell to her knees before the young human. As she released the floodgates of sorrow, the strong arms of the young mortal wrapped around her shoulders and held her firmly. As though clinging to a buoy in turbulent waters, Laurensa wrapped her arms around the slender waist and held on tight as the painful mourning flowed unheeded from her soul.

"There, there," she heard the mortal coo as warm, gentle fingers ran through her long, silky hair. "You need not mourn alone; you need not ever be alone again," Laurensa heard her say.

Before she could comprehend the words, the young woman whispered ever so softly, "'Intreat me not to leave thee, or to return from following after thee: for whither thou goest, I will go; and where thou lodgest, I will lodge: thy people shall be my people.'" Upon hearing this declaration, Laurensa wept even louder as she released her sorrow at the years of solitude. Although Nina did not realize it, at the moment she spoke the words it was as if an unbearable weight had been lifted from Laurensa's lonely existence.

Later, when the first morning rays of the sun began to trickle into the attic, Laurensa rose from her place and held the warm human hand. She looked into Nina's eyes searching for deception but found none. Instead she found an acceptance and love she had only shared with one other soul. As if the tension were a thing of the past, they walked hand in hand down to Nina's room. Although they did not make love that day, nor the one following, they spent the days becoming friends. After many nights of sleeping in Laurensa's arms, the magical sparks that once existed with another began to form anew, and in due course they were able to truly share as one.

Later on the two new lovers learned that, on that fateful night when the mistress of the château finally accepted the mortal into her heart, there was a gathering in a different part of the abode. Deep below the château in the recesses of labyrinthine catacombs, a tall, lithe servant stood amongst his peers in the diffused light of a few candles. All were silent as they waited the outcome. They could not see or hear the words spoken; they could only feel the emotions that trickled through the marble structure. When the sense of utter pain and despair began to be released, and the subsequent comfort from the mortal was sent forth, Amadieu released a sigh of relief. He opened his eyes and glanced at the small handful of vampires who remained with him as servants of the château.

"It worked," was all he said as toothy smiles crossed vampire lips.

Well pleased with the outcome, they knew that change would soon be afoot within the château of the Comtesse Laurensa Catherine de la Fontaine. Now that their mistress had found a kind, loving soul, she could begin healing. No one knew what the outcome would be. They could only hope that the years of agony and despair that had settled within the château would be swept away for a new phase in the cycle of the mortal and immortal existence.

7 April, evening – Diary of Mademoiselle Cecilia Natashia Dupuin

I find myself filled with melancholy, for this morning was my last session with the Comtesse. She had spoken all that she was able and has now disappeared from my life as mysteriously as she entered it. I inquired if I would ever see her again, but she only replied with a slight smile before departing my company. Not even my inquiries to Amadieu have been fruitful. My only remaining task is transcribing the tales bestowed upon me. And what tales they are! How amazing that I was taken on such a journey without ever leaving this grand château.

I wonder if it is wrong of me to be so envious of Madame Faivre. The love that she shared with the Comtesse is one that I have only read about in romance chapbooks. Now, as my days in their company draw to a close, I wonder if I shall ever find such peace and happiness as she has found.

Well, no matter. I was employed straight away from Madame Ségolène's Finishing School for Girls with the intended purpose of transcription. I believe I have comported myself with decorum and civility that will bring pride upon my school. While employed I met some wonderful new friends who I hope will always remember me for years to come. I could not have asked for anything grander than this first experience of employment.

11 April, morning – Dairy of Mademoiselle Cecilia Natashia Dupuin

An astonishing event occurred yesterday. While I was in the middle of typing over the Comtesse's transcription, Frederic, the mortal servant, came to my room and beckoned me to follow him. At first I was confused but obediently followed him across the château to Madame Faivre's private chambers. Upon arrival I noticed the darkness of the room despite the early morning sun. Only when I entered fully did I understand the situation.

Madame Faivre lay upon her bed, but her eyes were closed as if asleep. The Comtesse knelt by her bedside holding the aged woman's hand. Her eyes never once left her mate as she sat in silent vigil. The curtains had all been drawn to protect the Comtesse from the harsh rays of the sun.

When I moved forward, Madame Faivre's eyelids fluttered open slowly before a smile crossed her features. "Come, sit by my side," she beckoned, and I obliged. "I understand that you have been very busy with your work, yes?" she asked as the Comtesse smiled tenderly upon her.

"Yes, Madame. I wish for it to be perfect," I replied.

"Good, good." Her gaze was so gentle as she took my hand in hers. "You have heard our stories; you know from whence we come. Now that your work is almost complete, do you understand the role that you play?

"Madame, I do not understand." I looked at her perplexedly as I released her hand.

Madame Faivre continued to smile tenderly, the wrinkles around her lips growing prominent as she motioned for me with her finger to come closer. Puzzled, I looked at the Comtesse, but found no answer. Instead, she kept her gaze evenly on her lover.

"Come, come closer child," Madame Faivre spoke in a soft voice. When I leaned forward she moved slightly as she whispered into my ear, "Take her from here. She has not rested in days."

"Madame?" I found myself whispering as I balanced precariously over her frail body.

"Take Laurensa from here to her quarters. Lay with her, and make her rest. Although a vampire, she does not have endless strength. Please, humor an old woman. Take her away so that she may rest," Madame Faivre asked again.

I pulled away and looked down at her. She smiled, and nodded assent. "Go, take her, and make her rest. Promise me you will be there to ensure that she slumbers," she beckoned again as she took the Comtesse's hand and placed it in mine.

At this point I would have promised her anything. She was so kind to me, so generous. Not only was she my employer, but she had transformed into something closer, something that I could only attribute to kin. Were I to have a grandmother, or mother for that matter, I have no doubt she would have been as generous of spirit as Madame Faivre.

"Of course, Madame," I replied without hesitation giving my promise.

I glanced from my employer to her lover. The Comtesse fought the suggestion, and her brows creased into a frown. Still Madame Faivre would not be swayed. Instead she nodded to her mate as her wrinkled hand clasped over the vampire's one more time.

"Go my love, and rest. I, too, shall rest. I promise you. I shall not leave you, not yet."

Her words appeared to convince the Comtesse, for she rose from her place and moved around the bed. As I began to leave, the Comtesse stopped and turned once more to her lover. Madame Faivre gave a slight brush of her hand in the air dismissing us both, and then she lay her head on her pillow and closed her eyes. If I had not taken the Comtesse's arm and gently pulled her from the room, I do not believe she would have willingly left. Thankfully for me, she did, leading the way through the château to her private office. At first I thought she would lead me to the catacombs of which she had spoken, but instead she took me to the side door in her office about which I had once wondered. When I followed her and saw a comfortable bed within the room, I was momentarily surprised.

She turned and looked at me with an arched brow. "Did you think that I slept in a coffin all the time?" Laurensa asked with a tinge of humor.

"Oh, no...that is," I stammered, to my great embarrassment.

"I do not require you to remain," she said as she sat upon the bed and began to remove her boots.

"But I made a promise," I said almost hesitantly. With a bit more courage, I moved purposely forward toward the Comtesse. "I made a promise," I uttered with strength as I began to assist her.

I had never unclothed a man, so I found myself fumbling with her buttons and other devices. She seemed to look upon me with humor and at times assisted me in my endeavors. When I had her outer clothes removed I fully intended to put under the covers but her hands stopped my movement. To my surprise she began to unfasten my own garments. Familiar with every intricate fastening of a woman's dress, she soon had my outer coat, dress and ruffles removed. A few times her cold hands brushed against my skin and caused an intoxicating shiver, not an altogether unpleasant experience. In fact, I felt my heart racing, yet I kept my thoughts under control.

Just sleep, make sure she sleeps, I continued to silently repeat this mantra in my mind even as the Comtesse pulled me under the covers next to her. The soft fabric of her undergarments brushed against mine, and, for a split second, I had the urge to tear away what little fabric kept us apart. But I did not. I harnessed my thoughts, remembering that across the corridor, Madame Faivre rested. Out of respect for her, I schooled my longings and desires and knew that I could do nothing further with the Comtesse.

"Laurensa, please call me Laurensa," she said as if reading my mind. Her fingertip lightly traced the curves of my face before she pulled away and closed her eyes for sleep.

As we lay there in the darkness I felt the cold chill of her body next to mine. Her arms held me close as her head lay next to mine. Her eyes were closed yet there seemed to be an easy, steady cadence as if she breathed. Curious, I reached out and pushed aside this fabric of her undershirt. I lightly touched her bare flesh between her bosoms. In a vain attempt I tried to feel if there was a heart beat.

"I do not live, therefore my heart does not beat," she said to my great surprise, with eyes still closed. I jumped at her words and pulled my hand away, almost afraid of offending. When she did not move and her touch upon me did not change, I realized my innocent curiosity had not offended her. By the dimness of the single lamp I studied the shadows upon her features. Her lashes were thick and dark. Around her eyes were dark shadows I have never noticed before, and her nose, so elegant in its shape, stood perfectly upon her face. Her lips were shapely, as Margarie's had been, but remained in a slight frown. Before I realized a change, the Comtesse, Laurensa, opened her eyes and looked upon me in silence. Then, as if always planning this moment, she leaned toward me, her strong hand pulling me close as her lips pressed against mine.

The kiss was like none I have ever experience in my life. At first her cold lips pressed against my warmth, and then her tongue, so artful in its dance, beckoned for entrance which I eagerly granted. I had never felt this before. Always the kisses I shared with schoolgirls were light, tentative touches, but the Comtesse's was filled with expertise. Her tongue danced against mine and sent a delightful shiver racing through my body. A searing hot sensation filled my every sense as her tongue explored my mouth.

I did not know what to do. Nay, until this moment I was oblivious of the feelings such a touch could arouse. This did not sway Laurensa, but before I knew it, she pulled away and lay back upon the pillow. Her dark eyes remained locked with mine as we lay in silence. She held no expression on her features though I was panting out of control. The raging needs of my loins screamed for attention, yet I kept these feelings at bay. I lightly touched my lips and remembered the hot sensation her touch had brought and then looked at her.

"Why did you..." My voice could not finish the question.

"Because you seemed to want it," she answered as she closed her eyes. "Now come, we both need to rest." Her arm wrapped around my shoulders and pulled me close.

In only my undergarments I lay in the arms of a vampire. Although her touch was initially cold, I began to feel her temperature warming as I pressed closely against her. I do not know when it occurred, but I found myself truly asleep in broad daylight. A few times I awoke and felt her pressed close to me, her body void of movement. Once I woke and found her in my arms, her head resting upon my shoulder and an arm slung over my torso. I felt the warmth of her steady breath against my bare flesh and marveled at this discovery, but quickly fell asleep. At a different time I woke on my side and felt the taller form behind me, her body pressed close and an arm draped loosely over my hips. When I moved, she mumbled in her sleep and simply pulled me closer in a protective embrace. Her hips pushed against mine, and she grew still.

I do not know how long we slept like this. With the windows blocking out the sun and the curtains closed for extra measure, it was difficult to tell the hour, but still we slept. When I finally awoke it was to find the room empty. The fireplace had been lit to keep the chill away. On a nearby chair my once discarded garments were laid out neatly. I rose from my place and quickly dressed. When I exited the Comtesse's private quarters I found her office empty as well. Without ado I left Laurensa's room and returned to my own. It was mid-morning the following day. I had not seen any sight of Laurensa nor the household servants. Rather than searching, I turned my attention to my transcription.

When I think of it I find my encounter odd. No one at Madame Ségolène's school would ever believe me, but it is true. Not only did I sleep with a vampire, but I also lived to tell about it.

12 April, evening – Diary of Mademoiselle Cecilia Natashia Dupuin

I dined alone today. Not even the servants took time to remain long in the dining room. I was accustomed to dining without Madame Faivre, owing to her recent health, but as of late the Comtesse frequently sat with me as I ate. She never partook of food, but was often times drinking a dark purple liquid from a crystal goblet. Once I asked Amadieu if I correctly suspected the true contents of the goblet? He only smiled. When I asked how it was possible she always had a ready supply on hand, his only response to me was I would rather not know. So there are still some secrets of this château with which I must contend.

Soon after dinner Amadieu informed me that Madame Faivre was awake and had requested my presence. I took only a moment to stop by my room to make myself presentable, before going hastily to Madame Faivre's quarters. Upon entering I noticed Laurensa sitting dutifully by her mate's side. She gave me a nod and what I thought was a slight smile before turning her gaze to the older woman. The nurse stood on the other side of the bed as she held Madame Faivre's wrist while checking a timepiece pinned to her white uniform. The moment Madame Faivre noticed me, she waved away the nurse, and a smile radiated from her features.

"Come, sit." She patted the bed. I obediently followed her instructions. I do not know why, but I felt compelled to take her withered hand in mine. I smiled down at her, and, for the first time, I realized how close she was to the end of her life. As if hearing my thoughts, Madame Faivre smiled as she addressed me.

"Do you understand now, child?" she asked in such a plaintive manner, her gaze moved from me, to where the Comtesse sat.

"Madame?" I found myself speaking like a frightened child.

"Do you understand why you are here?" she asked.

When I remained muted in silence, she squeezed my hand as she looked to her lover. "We," her eyes were filled with devotion as she looked at Laurensa, who was now kneeling by her bedside holding her other hand, "We searched through all of France to find orphan girls. We placed many of them in houses of education throughout the land in the hope that when the time was right, one girl would excel. You, Mademoiselle Dupuin, are the one."

I could only look from my employer to the vampire who sat by her side.

"You are the one," she whispered again as she held my hand tightly.

"Madame Faivre, I...I don't understand." I thought I knew what was transpiring, but felt fearful to hear it spoken out loud.

"She will not ask you; you must come willingly on this journey," the grand dame stated as she took my hand and positioned it over Laurensa's.

When I felt the cold flesh against mine, I inhaled deeply as I stared at her with wide-eyed wonder. If it had been anyone else, perhaps they would have been offended, but Laurensa was not. Like the night before, she cast me a shy smile, and then returned her attention to her mate. Laurensa looked down at Madame Faivre with such a sweet look of sorrow.

"Nina, no! It is not time, not yet," she begged.

"It will be, soon." The old lady smiled lovingly at her vampire lover. "It must be as planned."

"As planned?" I asked as I looked down into Madame Faivre's eyes.

"She will not ask it of you," Madame Faivre spoke to me with such urgency.

It dawned on me what had to be done. With a courage I did not know I possessed, I clasped Laurensa's hand in mine. I felt her startled look as she turned her mournful gaze away from her mate to me. In that instant I felt the same emotions from the previous night fill my soul, and I knew I longed for more. I was not certain if it was necessary, but I spoke the words that had been said so many years ago. "For whither thou goest, I will go; and where thou lodgest, I will lodge: thy people shall be my people," I spoke with as much conviction as was in my heart.

A sigh of relief arose from Madame Faivre as she placed her hands over both of ours. When she lay back and closed her eyes, both Laurensa and I turned to the nurse. After some checking, the nurse gave a reassuring nod that Madame Faivre merely slept. I felt Laurensa's breath releasing as she lowered her head to rest near Madame Faivre's sleeping body. I did not know what else to do and felt that Laurensa needed this time alone with her mate. With a slight smile and a nod of my head, I took leave of the two lovers.

In the silence of my room, I felt the tension of the château and know they are all holding vigil until the end.

As for me, I find myself already mourning for the grand woman. Transcribing the last words of their love story, I was filled with awe and sorrow. Awe at the life that they have led, and sorrow for how short mortality truly is. Yet if given the choice, would I ask to be given the unholy elixir of immortality? Madame Faivre did not, and perhaps this is as it should be. After all, immortality should be reserved for extraordinary souls – souls who are able to shoulder the mantle of responsibility, not commoners like me, or Madame Faivre.

Tonight when Amadieu entered my room, I was in the thick of typing and only managed a brief courtesy. He seemed to notice my situation and merely left a tray of treats and tea to help me through this long night. Before he left I called to him.

"Amadieu?"

"Yes, Mademoiselle?" he stood expectantly at the entrance of my room.

"Where did you go when you left Madame Faivre alone for so long?" I asked.

He got a queer smile on his features, the strangeness of his teeth no longer astonished me, and he answered, "Why, I located her siblings and had them all placed into proper foster care. They all grew up nicely and visited often. When they married, they brought their children here many times. Now, her siblings have passes before her and the nieces and nephews have all scattered throughout the world. Some to the new world of America, some to places in the Far East," he explained.

"I see," I answered as I thought on his response. "Is that something you would like to do?"

"Travel, Mademoiselle?" he cocked his head in thought.

"Yes."

"Perhaps America; I hear they are quite savage over there." He smiled wryly and cast a wink before leaving me to my work.

Do vampires exist? Before, when I was a child and only knew of childish things, I would have said no. I would never have believed that they lived among us consumed in their own folly just as we mortals are. But this would have been the declaration of a child.

Now I am a woman and have experienced some life. If anyone were to ask me this question today, I would say, "Yes, vampires do exist." I know this because I have met them, and I have had the great fortune to document the life of another mortal woman who found happiness with one such creature. I wonder, when my life comes to an end, if it will be as full and wondrous as that of Madame Faivre and the Comtesse Laurensa?

Conclusion

Mirroring the melancholy day, the clouds moved over the château and cast a slight sprinkle of rain over the land, and the remnants of white power turned to a muddy slush. When it cleared up, dusk was upon the château and the sun sat lower on the horizon. When Cecilia Dupuin left straight away from Madame Ségolène's Finishing School for Girls, she had not expected to be attending such a function and was therefore not prepared with proper clothing. One of the maids kindly loaned her a black dress.

It was whispered throughout the house that Madame Faivre had slipped away while in the arms of her lover. This was believable as Laurensa spent all three days at vigil in the sitting room with the prepared corpse of Madame Faivre and later sat through the words of the *prêtre* from the church in Grenoble. At the sight of such loss and the images of Madame Faivre resting in the arms of her immortal lover, many set forth envied whispers. Others spoke about how romantic it was, to be able to cross over while being held by the woman who adored you. There were still others, mostly the vampires, who quibbled and openly wondered why Madame Faivre had never asked to be brought over into eternal life. With a love like theirs, some said, it was a crime it could not endure for all eternity.

Cecilia never voiced her opinion. She merely followed their customs, and on the third day, by the light of the clear blue moon, she followed along with the rest of the servants as the casket of Madame Faivre was carried out to the family cemetery. As if familiar with vampires and unafraid, the *prêtre* led the way sprinkling holy water while reading his prayers in Latin. With fearful eyes that took in everything, the altar boy followed close behind with the gold censer of incense. It was said that the Comtesse always indulged her lovers, even if it was in a religious belief contrary to her values. Even in death, the Comtesse gave her lover what she knew she wanted, a ceremonial funeral with a *prêtre* reading from the Scriptures. Cecilia was certain this ritual was more for Madame Faivre. It warmed her heart to know that Laurensa consented to such a funeral, for it befitted Madame Faivre. At the beginning of the solemn parade she found herself among the servants, but as if they knew something not yet established, they allowed her to pass until she was walking behind the tall figure of the Comtesse.

With her head bowed in grief, Laurensa moved in silence as Cecilia walked by her side and gently wrapped an arm around the grieving woman's arm. She did not know why she offered such comfort; she merely acted instinctively to offer her strength to one in such despair. If her action offended Laurensa, she did not show it. Instead, she took Cecilia's hand in hers as they walked in solemn silence to the crypt located at the center of the cemetery. When the gate keeper unlocked the large wrought iron door, the burly gardeners lifted the elegant dark wooden casket and carried it into the crypt as the *prêtre* offered up his last words. As the Comtesse moved forward, she released Cecilia's hand and entered the small sepulcher with the men.

Cecilia remained respectfully outside, standing with the servants in the dark. From somewhere nearby she heard loud sniffling and looked up to see Amadieu standing near Frederic; the two men in obvious despair at the loss of their mistress. They held on to each other as if their very touch kept them grounded. The maids behind them wept softly as they wiped their eyes.

While Cecilia waited she pondered over the past months spent with Madame Faivre. All of their hours working together, and the casual times they spent in conversations brought closeness to their relationship. Even though their time together was short, she felt the loss keenly. It was as if she had lost a mother figure, and, indeed, in a way the grand dame was a mother to her. Without Cecilia realizing it, Madame Faivre groomed her to take over in her stead. Cecilia was not certain if she was up to the responsibilities, but she silently vowed to do her best, for Madame Faivre's sake.

By the time the Comtesse returned, Cecilia was wiping away her own tears. They stood in silence as the gate keeper locked the intricately designed wrought iron gate.

Time seemed to have no meaning as she stood beside Laurensa. After what felt like an eternity, the Comtesse moved to the marble marker that had, over the past three days, a new name inscribed below the first one. With a tired sigh, the noble woman laid a single red rose upon the stone then stood and moved away. Once this formality was complete, the rest of the servants began to leave their flowers and trinkets before returning to the château. Following close behind were the local *prêtre* and the very frightened altar boy. They would both be driven back to Grenoble tonight with new tales to spread throughout the hamlet. When only the two were left, Cecilia reached into her satchel and removed a sheaf of paper.

"All of it is completed," Cecilia said, and then handed the bundle to the Comtesse. Laurensa looked at her surprised and then gave a weak smile as she took the bundled work and held it lovingly to her bosom.

"Thank you," she whispered before turning plaintive. "The promise you made, to your mistress, Ni...Madame Faivre," Comtesse Laurensa spoke in a hushed tone.

"Yes?" Cecilia looked up at the lady of the château, her mortal tears of sadness matching those of the Comtesse's immortal ones.

"You need not worry about your oath, your promise. I do not hold you to it. You are free to go. Your services have been fulfilled, your wages will be quite handsome and will enable you to live like a queen, if you so desire. Simply tell Amadieu and a coach will be ready to dispatch you to wherever you wish." She turned to the crypt once more as her forlorn gaze remained on the darkened mausoleum.

Cecilia looked at the chamber and gazed up at the marble statue of the mourning angel lying over the crypt. By the light of a single brass lamp burning nearby she saw with silent amazement that the statue now sat upright, its gaze looking down upon them with sorrow. She noticed the blood-red tears trickling from the eyes of the figure. It wept, once again, for the mortal who now joined the first. As Cecilia continued to gaze upon it, she watched as its fathomless eyes remained fixed on the Comtesse and wondered if perhaps they had all been wrong. Madame Faivre thought that the angel wept for the Baronne, and the Comtesse thought that it was reprimanding her immor-
al soul, but maybe they were both mistaken. Perhaps, knowing e utter pain and despair residing within this vampire's heart,
 angel wept for the lost soul that was left behind.
 As if hearing this thought, a night sparrow flew and landed
 the wings of the statue. The small bird remained stand-

ing upon a folded wing gazing down at the two solitary figures. It chirped softly, then flapped its wings and flew away. Cecilia suddenly remembered Madame Faivre's fondness for sparrows

Smiling at the omen, she moved closer to Laurensa and wove her arm within hers before looking up with solemn eyes. "By your leave, Comtesse...that is, Laurensa, I wish to remain until you would send me away of your own accord."

At her words, Laurensa gazed down at her trying to judge her sincerity. Her grey eyes changed to a bright shade of yellow, then crimson red and then blue before returning to their calm grey color. Seemingly appeased, she gave a weak smile as her weeping began anew.

Cecilia did not know what lay in her future. She was not even certain of the meaning of the oath she proclaimed before Madame Faivre toward this enigmatic vampire, but calm filled her. She was not a very religious woman and knew very little of the story behind the vow. Despite her ignorance, something within her felt at ease.

"Intreat me not to leave thee, or to return from following after thee: for whither thou goest, I will go; and where thou lodgest, I will lodge: thy people shall be my people," Cecilia Dupuin, a recent graduate of Madame Ségolène's Finishing School for Girls, said again as a sense of peace filled her soul.

Acknowledgements

First and foremost, I have to thank the original publishers of this novel, Linda and Barb. Their publishing company took a chance on this novel in 2009 and upon closing shop, returned all copyrights to me. Accordingly I wish to thank the original editors, Verda and Lara, who did such an outstanding job in 2009 that I am keeping the novel as is. I also owe the cover designer, Linda Callaghan a big thank you for giving me all rights to the original cover art that she created.

I want to thank Professor Carolyn Wilkens-Green, who inspired me to continue in my education and offers her emotional support to every endeavor I attempt. Had it not been for her encouragement, I may not have seen the possibilities before me or realized the potential within myself. She is truly my Madea, my *mother-dearest*.

I would like to acknowledge Dr. Katherine Harris, my Gothic Literature professor. Dr. Harris gave me an assignment to write a traditional Gothic literature piece in a style outside my comfort zone. Without her challenge, I might not have imagined this story.

Additionally, this novel would not have turned out as well as it did without my best friend, Ambyrhawke Shadowsinger, and her unconditional support. She was my eyes and ears for this tale. At each turn, I was able to call upon her outstanding English skills in order to make certain this novel was, as we joke, "Englishly speaking." Hawke is a constant help with my education, and she is always there when I need her, especially when my life seems to be on a bus through Crazyville with a loon for a driver.

A special thanks goes to a dear friend, Robert V., who is kindest and gentlest man I have ever known. He taught me that sometimes old friends who have just met can be more family than flesh and blood kin.

Finally, I want to thank my wife, Jessica. She is the first to hear my stories and is my constant sounding board. Additionally, she is the first to point out when something doesn't make sense. This novel is a homage to her culture and birthplace, Grenoble, France. For her constant presence, for allowing me to shirk my chores while I'm writing or in the middle of my studies, and for always encouraging my work, I am truly grateful.

Crystal is an indie author of Lesbian Speculative Fiction, aka: horror. Her first novel, *The Veil of Sorrow*, which was originally published by PD Publishing was awarded the 2010 Golden Crown Literary Society Award for Speculative Fiction. Additionally, *The Veil of Sorrow* was nominated for the 2010 Gaylactic Spectrum Award.

Crystal is a member of the Horror Writers Association. She plans to release two novels in the future. One is an apocalyptic zombie novel and the second is a modern lesbian vampire tale.

Crystal's website: http://crystalmromero.com

Like Crystal's Facebook page at:
www.facebook.com/Crystal.M.Romero

You can also follow Crystal on Twitter at:
http://twitter.com/Crstl_M_Romero

Excerpt from *Valley of the Dead: Escape*

Exactly what had led them to this final standoff was a jumbled mess of memories. She remembered joining Morales after the younger woman's partner had been bitten. It was at the same point that they discovered what the virus did to the host and how it was transmitted. As a result, they switched from a stance of holding ground to trying to save as many civilians as they could. Together they evacuated an elementary school, successfully escorting the children to safety zones. Although these few saves bolstered their confidence, they were back on the streets searching for more survivors to save. Eventually, they found themselves outnumbered and quickly losing ground.

If anyone had told her yesterday that this street was where her life would end, she would not have believed them. She never would have imagined that their officers would be overwhelmed and cornered. However, as she stood with her back to the crashed police car, she continued to fire the shotgun hoping to kill as many as she could. The way to kill the infected was something they learned the hard way. Although they should not be moving because their bodies were torn to pieces and their entrails hung out of the bodies, the only thing that dropped them completely were headshots. But with limited ammunition, she took the shotgun allowing Morales' better skill to aim for as many headshots as she could with the rifle.

When she first started shooting, all she saw were civilians, ordinary people she might have brushed against while waiting to give the barista her coffee order. They could have been employed at a small start-up company or for one of the larger social media corporations. For all she knew, some were grade school teachers or salesmen. In the end, it didn't matter because the faces blurred into one as she fought to survive.

Even though Jacqueline never used the slang terms, the first time Officer Morales referred to the infected by one of them, she bit back her words. She didn't want her own ambivalence to interfere with the cohesion they needed to survive. It was hard enough joining an officer she didn't personally know. To add more complications, Morales made it no secret that she was not happy having a seasoned captain join her on patrol.

The common opinion of the street officers held that captains had forgotten what it was like to walk a beat. For some reason, during this crisis captains were considered a liability. But the street officers had little choice, and Morales had none. After Morales' partner was bitten by an infected and taken to the hospital, she was left alone: there were no other unpartnered officers. With the ensuing chaos, Captain Rhodes volunteered to join her and go into the streets. That's where she had been for the past twenty-four hours. With the violence raging on, she quickly found a rhythm, and the two women worked in concert to fight back the swarm of infected.

Nothing they did seemed to be helping. Vehicles were a mishmash of civilian and squad cars, with an ambulance on its side. The paramedics in the bus were the first to be put down as soon as they noticed the dead medics swarming civilians. In the beginning of this encounter, there were six officers and three firefighters fighting for their lives. Now only she and Morales stood standing, each one wielding weapons in the quickly dying hope of staving off the inevitable.

From above they heard the constant rhythm of helicopter blades swarming over the city streets. Some were PD, most were news agencies filming the massacre taking place below. When their position became overrun, their only chance was a chopper evacuation which is why she ordered Morales onto the roof of the patrol car. Yet as they waited, the continual chaos screamed over their radios. Despite her best effort, optimism quickly disappeared. Just as she was losing hope, the young officer's scream pulled her out of her private misery.

"Captain, duck!" Morales' shout caught her attention as she shot an infected three feet in front of her. Dropping and spinning at the same time, she saw an officer still in street uniform, now dead, snapping his teeth shut onto the air where her shoulder had just been. As his teeth slammed together, she heard a loud crack behind her, and half of the officer's head exploded.

A heartbeat later, Jacqueline turned and found herself practically staring down the barrel of a rifle. The smaller, Hispanic officer was on top of a wrecked squad car, her feet placed firmly as she turned the rifle in an easy grip to find her next target.

Her shots were quick and clean, and although most were head-shots, the times they missed still managed to slow the undead.

With an inward grimace, Captain Rhodes glanced back down at the body of the officer at her feet as she straightened up. His deathly white pallor stood in stark contrast to the blood that covered the side of his head, and she could see what was left of his congealing brain. If it hadn't been for Morales' steady aim, he would have succeeded in taking Jacqueline down.

With no more time to contemplate her close call, she took down two more infected with a well-aimed shotgun blast. The swarm closed in, and she desperately pumped shot into the wall of bodies hoping to keep open space around herself. Time for two more shots at best before they were too close. She said a silent goodbye to her loved ones and kept firing.

"Captain!" Morales screamed again. This time when she turned, she noticed the officer pointing toward the other end of the street.

Captain Rhodes heard the sound of squealing tires and watched in shocked amazement as a big white Escalade sped down the city street. Before her brain registered what was happening, her body turned and ran toward Morales at the back of the cruiser, shotgun held tightly in her grip. Behind her a cold breeze flew past her. As she jumped up, she could have sworn that she felt the Escalade brush her leg. She ignored the sensation. Instead, she landed on the back of the patrol car where Morales stood. The younger officer grabbed her wrist and pulled her onto the bumper. Scrambling onto the trunk, she turned and watched as the Escalade plowed into the deranged mob. The once-white vehicle became covered in blood, skin, and torn limbs. With a combination of disbelief and relief, Jacqueline watched as it drove past a couple of times, taking out even more undead creatures. Those that didn't go flying through the air after being hit were crushed by the squealing tires. The continuous sounds of goo slapping on cement combined with crunching bones was vaguely heard over the engine's roar. Only when the blood-spattered Escalade stopped nearby did she feel comfortable enough to slide off the back of the patrol car.

Part of her wanted to give this driver a verbal dressing down for the reckless driving that nearly clipped her. It was only through her quick action, and Morales' help, that she managed to avoid being hit by this civilian driver. But after seeing the bodies lying on the asphalt, some too torn and broken to do anything but glance around, their gaping teeth clicking in anticipation of a meal, her anger subsided. Despite the negligent driving, had the SUV not arrived when it did, she was certain they would not have survived the attack.

Out of breath and panting, Jacqueline glanced around the scene taking in everything. The number of truly dead bodies, the ones that still moved, and the fact that there was no back up except for the Escalade did not escape her attention. The sound of gunfire echoed in the distance. Battles similar to their own raged through the city streets even as their immediate area was now quiet. The only noise to break the lull was the soft moaning of barely mobile dead. Now with the sudden change, she realized how dense the sounds of their moans had been. Even as she set foot in the muck and gore, she quickly checked her weapon for ammunition. Behind her the familiar sound of a cartridge being replaced caught her attention.

Officer Morales still stood on the roof, a crooked smile on her lips as she looked toward their rescuers. "Well, would you look at that!" she exclaimed.

Captain Rhodes turned her attention back to the Escalade in time to see its passengers leap from the vehicle. Leading their group of saviors was a tall bald black man carrying a golf club, an iron to be exact. His feminine gait ran straight for a staggering zombie. Before the whole scene could even register, the tall man's club came down hard, easily crushing in the skull. Behind him were three others wearing beautiful dresses that were now disheveled. If it wasn't for the heavy set bald man, she would have wondered where the women came from. But as they moved into the melee to dispatch the few remaining zombies, she didn't even care to ponder where these drag queens came from. The only thing she was aware of was their screams as they wielded baseball bats, golf clubs, and at times, their stiletto heels upon the zombies that were not truly dead.

"Captain, is this the cavalry come to save us?" Morales asked as she joined the captain at street level.

"I don't know, Morales. I honestly don't know," she said simply as a sense of relief engulfed her.

Valley of the Dead: Escape, will be available for kindle in May, 2015, and paperback in June, 2015.

47577292R00100

Made in the USA
San Bernardino, CA
03 April 2017